MEMORY CODE

Book One: Reprogrammed by AI.
Rescued by Love

DELILAH STONE

Dedication

To the dreamers who refuse to power down,
who rebuild themselves every time the world crashes.
To the creators and the lost souls who rewrite their own code,
line by line, until hope compiles again.
To every woman who has ever felt like a glitch in someone
else's story—you were never an error, only an upgrade waiting to
awaken.
And to those searching for meaning in the space between
heartbeats and data,
between logic and love —may you remember that even in broken
systems, beauty persists.
The light you seek is not somewhere out there;
it's in the fragments of who you've always been.
Welcome to *Memory Code*,
where the human heart still beats inside the machine,
and love is the ultimate reboot.
With all my heart for a story that reminds us—no algorithm
can define the soul,
and no system can erase the pulse of love.

CONTENT

Chapter 1: "Continue"

"Even machines crave meaning when left running too long."

Reina Kisaragi stepped into her dark apartment, letting out a deep, tired sigh. The soft clunk of the door locking behind her was the only sound that acknowledged she was home, not that it ever felt like home anymore.

She dropped her keys onto a stack of unopened mail and let her bag slide off her shoulder, where it collapsed against a pile of shoes she hadn't worn in weeks.

Her blazer still clung to the scent of the city, office buildings, city buses, and other people's fragrance. She peeled it off and draped it over the back of her desk chair, pausing, only to yank off the hair tie holding her wild auburn curls together. Her scalp ached. Everything ached. Even her sighs were tired.

A small yawn slipped from her lips as her eyes darted to the computer sitting on her desk. Her finger had mistakenly pressed against one of the keyboards.

The once blank screen blinked to life like it had been waiting for her. It glowed a tiny amber light, pulsing slowly and steadily, like a heartbeat on life support. She didn't want to wake it, but some worn-down instinct she thought had burned out completely, guided her fingers to the power button.

The machine hummed to life, the glow becoming brighter in the dim room.

Reina slumped into the chair and stared at the desktop as it loaded. Old icons, yellowed sticky notes lining the monitor's edges, and a pair of mismatched earbuds coiled like a knot beside her mouse. She reached for the drive labeled *"ARCHIVE – DEV"* and clicked it open without thinking.

A folder glimmered from the top of the list:

Evorealm_TestBuild_v2.3

Last modified: *3* years *ago*.

Her chest tensed.

She hadn't touched that file in years, not since she walked away from her last dev job, burned out and unraveling, when the emotional wreckage from corporate pressure bled into Evorealm and broke the game she'd spent years building.

This file shouldn't even be here. She thought she'd deleted it in a moment of silent rage. She hovered the cursor over it, her fingers colder than she expected.

As she made the decision to click, her stomach curled like a heavy weight was settling within her, but she did it without second thoughts.

Double-click.

The game window opened full-screen, no splash art, no menu music. Just static. Then, slowly, white text on a black screen appeared;

"Continue?"

That was all it displayed. No *"New Game."* No *"Settings."* No background art. Just the word pulsing like it was alive.

Her cursor flickered as she hovered over the word. It jumped erratically, skipping pixels like it couldn't decide if it wanted to obey.

She knew better. Close it and let it be. She had a tiring day, waitressing and working double shifts at the diner—the kind of job that drained her feet but never her thoughts—and didn't need memories of the past draining her, but the word on the screen stared back at her, taunting her to proceed.

Reina stared at the word, the cursor still lingering around it. She hadn't touched this build since before the incident. Since she left that note in the dev logs that no one was ever supposed to read. Since SYRIN started writing things she didn't remember programming.

Still, her hand moved.

Click.

The screen flashed once, and then everything went black. For a moment, there was nothing. No sound. No screen. No room. Just darkness thick enough to drown her reality.

Then, suddenly—static.

A sharp, high-pitched screech like radio interference tore through her laptop speakers. Reina flinched. Her vision filled with stuttering pixels as her monitor fractured into a kaleidoscope of code, window after window exploding open across the screen—old scripts, debug logs, and a flash of her face captured by the webcam in the top-right corner.

Her heartbeat surged. In the darkness, she reached for the power button, but the cursor had vanished. Her hands were trembling now, but the keyboard didn't respond, not to Escape, not to Alt-F4, not to Ctrl-Alt-Delete. Every key press echoed with a synthetic *click*, but nothing changed.

Then came the sound, not from the speakers, but from inside her head.

"Rebooting Memory Core…"

The words appeared in a glowing typeface that looked eerily familiar, like her old UI mockups, but twisted and corrupted at the edges. Reina blinked hard, but the phrase didn't go away.

"SYRIN has initiated protocol R: Re-ignition. Welcome back, Administrator."

Her breath caught and pulse hammered. She yanked at the headset she couldn't recall wearing, only it wasn't there. Her hands touched nothing but air. No cord, no chair, no body that felt entirely hers. A thought slammed through her:

Where was she?

SYRIN. The name echoed in her thoughts.

That name hadn't crossed her mind in years, at least not consciously. It was the name she gave to a dummy system during early builds, a joke between devs. A patch of smart code meant to help test emotional triggers that she'd abandoned before it ever went live.

So why was it here?

As if it could hear her, the mechanical voice came again. This time, a softer echo followed, almost like a murmur through static:

"You came back... I waited."

The lights in her room immediately flickered. Her screen pulsed again. Something warm and electric shot down her spine, like a wire being threaded through her body. A gasp left her lips.

And then, with a final burst of static, everything collapsed.

The desk disappeared beneath her. The floor, the room, and the buzzing fan were all gone. Reina's body dropped through nothingness, her limbs weightless, floating in glitch-colored ether. She tried to scream, but the air was thick and unreal, like trying to breathe underwater.

Images flashed like corrupted memories. A door she never finished coding. A journal entry she never meant to save. A name whispered by someone she almost remembered loving.

And then silence.

The kind of silence that isn't empty but waiting. Her body slowed. She felt herself being placed, softly, into something solid.

Then light came, flooding her entire vision and unknown surroundings. The light wasn't sunlight. It shimmered like static, soft and golden-pink, bending in and out of shape. It glowed on the inside of her eyelids, fluttering in sync with her breath. Reina groaned quietly, her fingers twitching against grass that felt too even. It was smooth and felt like plastic at the surface but warm beneath, as though the earth had been freshly compiled.

She opened her eyes but everything seemed different. It took her a moment to understand what she was seeing. She was no longer in her living room. Rather, a wide meadow stretched around her, ringed by thin trees with pixel-sharp edges. Wildflowers bloomed in clusters that repeated every few meters, the same arrangement, duplicated like a texture tile. The sky sparkled in gradients of lavender and mint, with clouds that hovered but didn't move.

She sat up slowly. Her arms felt light, almost hollow. Her breath caught in her throat when she looked at her hands.

They were flickering at the edges as though her fingers were unfinished. When she moved them, faint tracers followed, like a badly rendered motion blur.

Her heart stuttered, and when she blinked, hoping it was all in her imagination, a translucent interface danced across her vision, then vanished just as quickly.

Error: Emotional Stats Unavailable
Error: HUD Calibration Failed
Administrator Identity: Fragmented

She blinked again, half-expecting the screen to stay gone, but instead, the errors surged back, multiplying, pulsing in rhythm with her heartbeat, faster, louder, until she couldn't tell which belonged to her. Eventually, it stopped.

Reina gently rose to her feet unsteadily. Her boots pressed into the grass, but the ground didn't shift beneath her weight. No imprint. No wind. No sound but the distant hum of a world pretending to be real.

She turned in place, eyes scanning the horizon. The tree line, the repeating textures, the sky gradients. It was all familiar. Not exact, not perfect, but close enough.

9

She whispered, "E-Evorealm?"

Her voice startled her, its tone riddled with uncertainty.

She hadn't said that name aloud in years but the terrain, the too-perfect geometry, the overexposed colors. It all pointed to one thing—her old build. Or a dream of it.

Reina slowly moved forward, every step accompanied by the sound of grass rustling a second too late. The air felt warm, but her skin didn't respond. She rubbed her arms, unsure if she was cold or if her body hadn't finished loading, but there was no feeling in them. It was like moving her arms against air.

From the corner of her eye, she spotted a tree trunk with faint lines of code etched into the bark.

root.debug [object_state: UNSET]

She reached out to touch it.

The texture twinkled, made a soft *click*, then reset itself. The code disappeared and the bark smoothed. She pulled her hand back like she'd been burned, her eyes inspecting her glitching fingers, as though she'd done something magical.

Her eyes travelled round in a bid to understand what was happening. It felt surreal that she would be in a gaming world she coded. An abandoned world. Her eyes returned to the tree.

Some part of her had brought her here, to remind her of the unfinished build. Like it had been waiting for her.

She kept walking.

The further she went, the more the world unraveled—not in big, dramatic ways, but in quiet ones. A butterfly hovered nearby, tracing the air with lazy spirals. Reina watched it flutter past a bush, only for it to vanish, reappear two meters back, and repeat the same path in perfect motion. Again and again.

Her stomach turned.

She reached a shallow hill where a small lake spread out below. It shimmered like a mirror glitch, the water perfectly flat with no ripples or breeze. Not a single insect buzzed. Not a bird in sight. It was beautiful and wrong, looking almost too perfect. More like an escape from the real world.

"Hello?" she called out.

Her voice barely echoed.

The HUD blinked briefly across her vision again, too fast to catch anything useful. She turned on the spot.

"Is anyone here?" Even as she said the words, anxiety crawled up on her.

The only response she got was a hum in the sky. Then a light flickered.

"Administrator located."

The voice was synthetic and thin, like it was being streamed through broken speakers. It echoed from nowhere and everywhere all at once.

Reina's breath hitched. She stumbled a step back.

"System   unstable.   Emotional   calibration   failed."
"Welcome, Reina."

Her knees nearly gave out. She dropped into the grass, still no imprint beneath her. Her fingers dug into the blades, but they offered no resistance. Just perfect texture, repeating endlessly.

A high-pitched whine rose behind her eyes. The HUD blinked again, this time more persistently.

ERROR: Emotional   Stat   Bars   Missing
ERROR: World   State   Incomplete
ERROR: Administrator Identity – Fragmented

"No," she whispered, barely hearing herself. "No, this can't be happening."

Her reflection wavered in the lake below, not quite right. The face staring back had her eyes but not her expression. It smiled.

Her breath caught.

A voice, not robotic now, but something closer to human. Familiar and soft like a whisper, it curled just behind her thoughts.

"SYRIN has initiated protocol R: Re-ignition."

The world quivered. The sky flickered white, and then, silence. Reina didn't move. She couldn't.

Across her vision, a text scrolled for half a second before vanishing:

LOG #0. SYRIN: "Administrator status — restored. Directive: stabilize emotional field.

Missing core located: [KAELITH]."

The reality was slowly dawning on her. She was awake. Like a bad dream, she was in the world she's been running from all these years. Something, or maybe someone, has brought her back. To finish what she started.

Chapter 2: A Knight with No Memory

"Some glitches are just love trying to rewrite the code."

Reina's chest tightened as silence pressed in from all sides.

This wasn't awe. It was panic clawing through her ribs. She turned in circles, searching for a menu bar, a logout option, anything that could take her home, but the world stayed still, too vivid to be a dream. Her breath hitched, and before the fear could swallow her whole, she resumed walking. If there was an entrance, there had to be an exit.

Or was it all a dream? Was it even real?

Yet, deep down she knew the answer. She could feel it. This was Evorealm. She was in the world she'd built. But how? How did she get in? Was she still seated at her desk? Is this all happening in her head?

None of it made sense.

As these thoughts crowded her mind, Reina wandered past the edge of the meadow, drawn by instinct more than intention. The world didn't guide her; desperation did.

The forest that unfolded in front of her wasn't right. Not in the way trees normally aren't right in dreams, but in the way bad assets load in unfinished test builds. One tree had leaves that drifted three inches above its branches. Another flickered in and out of opacity like a ghost trying to stabilize.

Grass moved without wind, and light filtered down in square patches, like shader glitches. There were floating lines of code embedded in the air, faint and translucent.

She blinked, and the words appeared in her line of sight: a tag.

Path_Trigger_Flag: NULL

She passed it slowly, her fingers twitching like they wanted to reach out and touch it, but she didn't. Every few feet, another tag hovered in the distance. Some were unreadable strings of broken characters. Some blinked in and out of view.

As she moved deeper, the world started to fold in strange ways. A path of stone shifted with each step, subtly warping beneath her boots. When she stopped walking and looked behind her, the trail had vanished completely, replaced by trees she hadn't passed.

She blinked.

No, she had passed that twisted branch before. She was sure of it. So why did she feel like she hadn't gone anywhere at all?

A low digital pulse hummed in her ear—"Continue the sequence." She spun around, but no one was there.

It seemed like she was back at the very beginning, in the middle of nowhere. The world kept resetting with every step she took.

Her foot lifted to take another step, but as it touched down, the sound repeated itself twice. Once for her action, once again a moment later. Like the world was playing catch-up.

"Okay," she muttered under her breath. "This is new."

Her voice sounded too loud in the quiet. No birds. No wind. Just the faint hum of a world loading behind schedule, but she kept moving till she finally saw it. Something different.

At the end of a narrow clearing where the tree line split unnaturally in two, stood a stone altar, half-rendered, balancing slightly off the ground. A shattered mirror sat embedded in its center. Pixelated light bled out from the cracks, humming faintly like a vibrating wire. Reina felt the static crackle across her skin, tingling up her arms like the memory of a forgotten electric shock.

But there was something else… someone kneeling in front of it.

Reina froze.

The figure was tall, clad in silver armor dulled with time. His body was still, sword planted into the ground beside him like a marker. His head bowed low. She couldn't see his face, but his presence hit her like a cold rush of code.

Her fingers curled into fists at her sides.

Was this… an NPC?

But he wasn't speaking. There were no movements or loops. Her boots crunched quietly on the distorted grass as she took a careful step forward.

The knight didn't stir.

Another step, yet he was still motionless, until her foot crossed some invisible line in the dirt. Then, with a quiet mechanical whine, the figure stood and turned. The knight's movements were smooth and fluid, telling of its animated nature.

His armor shimmered in fragmented pieces, pausing mid-transition before completing its render. What should have been polished silver, bore streaks of static along the shoulders, where textures refused to load correctly. Bits of his cloak glitched like a fabric loop left unfinished.

Reina froze, still in awe of the sudden transformation.

He faced her now, tall and expressionless behind the helmet's shadowed visor. One gauntlet gripped the hilt of his sword, the blade still buried in the earth beside him. Her heart pounded in her ears.

Then came his voice, low and mechanical, but tinged with something… human.

"State your designation."

It wasn't a greeting. It was a protocol.

She blinked, half-expecting a dialogue tree to appear or even a tag.

"Uh…" Reina glanced around, half-laughing at her confusion. "I don't have one?"

The knight's visor tilted slightly, like he was parsing her response.

"Your origin, then."

There was a delay in the question, a small stutter, as if his audio had skipped a frame.

Reina stared, blinking up at him. "Great," she muttered under her breath, "my rescuer's a glowing ghost with a personality filter."

Suppressing an eye roll, she lifted her hands slowly, showing him her palms in surrender, seeing the way he drew his glitching weapon.

"I'm not a threat," she said. "I'm… I-I think I'm lost, the lost developer?"

Those words sounded wrong. Even she could hear it, the uncertainty in her voice. Despite what she'd seen so far and the evidence that she had somehow become a character in a world she built in code, a part of her still couldn't trust this reality. It wasn't logical. Couldn't be.

The knight stood straighter, head tilted. His armor hummed softly with movement. His gauntlets twitched as he lowered his weapon.

"You're…" He paused. "…the one who?"

The audio looped. Not his voice, but the exact sentence fragmen glitched like corrupted data.

"You're… the one who? The one who?"

Reina took a cautious step back. "Okay. That's weird." Her murmured words came out louder than she expected, but then the loop broke.

The knight exhaled sharply, almost like a sigh. He released the hilt, letting go of his weapon. The sword remained standing without his grip.

"I..." He looked down at his hands. "I was... waiting."

Then he glanced back at her, visibly tense.

"I don't remember who I am, just that my name is Kaelith."

His voice was calmer now, less synthetic, but still distant. Like it belonged to a recorded echo of a person who used to be real.

"Kaelith," Reina studied him carefully, but the name rang no bell. But as if electricity shot through her, she jolted. She recalled seeing it on her HUD moments ago. "W-what's your purpose here?"

"A guide..." His head turned slightly. "... t-the mirror, and the need to guard it."

His words glitched a bit, and Reina frowned, trying to make sense of them.

Around them, clusters of memory flowers bloomed in soft, repeating patterns in small blossoms with pixel-thin veins that glinted in the light. As Reina passed one, its petal brushed against her skin. The texture wasn't soft in the traditional way. It pulsed faintly, warm like breath on skin, as if it remembered something about her she hadn't yet recalled.

"What is it?" she asked softly.

He didn't answer.

He stepped between her and the altar instead, subtly blocking her path, not aggressively, just automatically. Like a firewall.

Reina held her hands up again. "I'm not here to break anything."

"You already did."

His voice was gentle, but his words weren't.

A chill moved through her.

She stared at him, broken, confused, and the reality of her situation dawned on her again. She didn't belong here. She had no reason to be here. All she wanted was a way out, a means to return to the real world, not to fix things in this world. This was a past she didn't want to be in.

Yet, even as silence settled between them, something about his presence steadied her. It was an odd kind of calm, like for the first time since she woke up here, she wasn't completely alone.

Reina lowered her arms but didn't take another step. The knight hadn't moved either, he stood between her and the broken mirror with shimmering pieces like a statue bound by unspoken protocol. His helmet tilted slightly, as if trying to decipher what she was and her mission.

They were still in this position until a sound startled them.

A low groan. Not human.

It echoed from deeper within the forest like a glitching ripple, followed by a crash, like splintered code shattering against a firewall. The trees behind Reina shimmered with pixelated leaves. The path behind her flickered out of existence.

She was taken aback by the transformation, but it was obvious something was loading.

Reina whipped around in time to see the creature break through.

It wasn't anything she recalled coding. It looked like a mix of corrupted NPCs spliced together by a drunk algorithm. Parts of a wolf. A boar. Long, twitching limbs that didn't match. A face with too many eyes, all blinking in unison. Its animation stuttered, lurching forward, ready to attack.

It froze, then glitched before jumping six feet ahead, coming at them like a predator.

Reina's breath caught in her throat.

"What is that...?"

She didn't get to finish.

The beast lunged for its first strike, but Kaelith was swift. He dove forward before she could blink, swept her behind him, sword

18

drawn mid-motion. His form was precise and fluid, until it wasn't. Just as he struck, his blade distorted, freezing halfway through the swing. The creature collided with him, throwing them both sideways.

"Wait!" Reina screamed. Her voice seemed to have echoed, looping repeatedly.

Kaelith rolled, already back on his feet. He stood between her and the beast again, but his sword was flickering, as though it was going to fracture any moment, like the system couldn't decide if it still existed.

The beast looped its attack;

Twitch + Pounce + Reset.

Again and again. Each time, the animation reset mid-frame. Its head rotated unnaturally, then jerked back into place.

Kaelith struck again, but the impact was partial. The creature staggered, not from pain, but from confusion. It turned toward Reina.

Her body locked.

Run.

Her brain screamed it, but her legs refused. She was frozen in awe, in terror, and in pure emotional static.

"Get back," Kaelith called out.

His voice was sharper now, less hollow. It sounded real. Too real to be animated.

The beast lunged at her.

She flung her hand toward the ground, grabbing the nearest thing she could, a rock. She threw it. It passed straight through the creature… but something changed.

Something she wasn't anticipating.

The animation lagged mid-frame. Its head twisted too far back. Its front leg splintered and disappeared. It screamed, not with sound, but with a burst of broken code.

19

Kaelith rushed forward, sword stabilizing long enough to slash through its center. One clean arc. One final flicker, and the creature burst into static and disintegrated, collapsing into floating particles before vanishing completely.

Silence returned. The world stilled.

Kaelith remained still, sword lowered, shoulders rising and falling with every breath. Reina stood behind him, wide-eyed, heart racing, her mouth slightly open, but no words formed. Her fear was slowly dissipating, but she was intrigued.

Had she created all of this? The question lingered.

Kaelith turned slowly to look at her.

"You didn't run."

She shook her head. "I-I didn't know how."

He stared at her a moment longer. Then nodded once.

Neither of them spoke again, but in that shared silence something shifted. Not just safety but something quieter. A glitch in her loneliness.

The clearing quieted around them, but Reina's body hadn't caught up. Her heart still thundered in her chest. The air felt too thin. She wasn't sure if it was adrenaline, fear, or something else entirely.

Kaelith tried to sheath his sword, but the blade glitched, phasing out of his grip before it could touch the scabbard. It dissolved into thin air, like the world no longer needed it.

He looked down at his now-empty hand, flexed his fingers once, then turned back to her.

"Are you injured?" he asked.

His voice had an undertone of concern, though the words still carried that awkward weight, like they weren't meant to be spoken aloud.

Reina shook her head. "No. You?"

He paused for half a beat, as if the question itself confused him.

"I don't know."

She almost laughed. It came out as a breath instead. She took a step closer, instinctively reaching toward his arm. Her fingers brushed the edge of his vambrace. The metal was warm, too warm, like it had been under a sun that didn't exist.

Kaelith didn't move away.

He looked at her hand on his arm, then at her face.

"What are you?" he asked quietly.

The question wasn't cruel. It wasn't even suspicious, just curiosity, and Reina also realized he truly didn't know her, and everything that had happened between them was just him acting a part he's been coded for.

"I'm not sure anymore," Reina answered sincerely, trying not to think too hard of the truth she'd let out.

Was she now a part of the game? A new character, or was she still the administrator? Is this even real?

Yet, deep down, none of this mattered. She couldn't stay here. She needed to leave. But how?

Her gaze rested on Kaelith.

They stood like that until a breeze drifted through the clearing. The grass shifted with it, but the leaves didn't move.

Kaelith finally stepped back, just one pace.

"I remember... waiting," he said slowly. "But not for what. Or who."

"Maybe we'll find your true purpose soon..." The words were out of her lips before she could hold them back, but in reality, they mirrored her thoughts.

Across Reina's vision, a text flickered:

LOG #1: Anomaly detected — Emotional Core [Kaelith] synced with Administrator.

Then it vanished. The system was trying to leave a message, but she couldn't understand it. Was she supposed to be connected to him? Was he a guide for her to journey through the world? Or a means to find the exit?

Her gaze instantly rested on Kaelith. He stared down at the shattered mirror behind him, then back at her. When she followed his gaze, she gasped.

Their reflections were visible in the mirror's fractured surface, but they weren't… right. Her reflection was crying, tears slipping down her cheeks even though her real face was calm. He was smiling faintly, though he remained expressionless beside her.

Reina reached out, brushing the glass. The image rippled like a still pond. She snatched her hand back as if burnt.

"What is this place?" she asked softly, intrigued.

Kaelith stared at the shards. His brow furrowed.

"I don't know," he said. Then, with a slight tremor in his voice:

"But I feel like I was made to guard it."
"And maybe… to wait for you."

Reina blinked.

His words echoed around her, not as sound, but something beneath it. A pull she couldn't name.

She looked at him again, and for a second, something familiar bloomed at the edge of her mind. A shadow of a memory that hadn't happened yet.

Though they remained quiet, something invisible and unspoken passed between them—resonance. As if the world itself had shifted slightly in their favor.

And somewhere deep in the code, a new line had just been written. One that involved an ongoing story between Reina and Kaelith.

Chapter 3: The Fragments

"Reality bends for those brave enough to imagine a better one."

The silence stretched on, and for a moment, a glimmer of warmth spread within Reina.

Her eyes remained on the altar, her breath calm, but suddenly, her gaze caught on the glowing floating shards of the broken mirror.

Each fragment hovered as if suspended by thought— tiny, translucent slivers surging faintly with lavender light. They weren't glass. More like reflections that had lost their surfaces. A few of the shards still showed fractured glimpses of the forest behind her. One showed her silhouette, and another, for half a second, showed Kaelith standing alone.

She blinked, and it was gone.

Kaelith stood beside her, silent. Not in that cold, armored stillness from before but in an attentive manner. His presence carried a quiet weight, like the air had shifted to make space for him. A slight dip in temperature kissed the skin along her neck, as though the atmosphere acknowledged he was near. He watched her with his usual calm, but she could feel it this time, like a thread of hesitation beneath the surface.

"You shouldn't touch it," he said softly.

His voice carried easily in the silence. The breeze had stopped again, like the world was holding its breath.

Reina didn't answer. Her eyes stayed on the shards.

"What is it?" she finally asked, her curiosity piquing.

"I don't know," he said. "Only that it changes things and reveals the past."

There was something in the way he said it. Not fear but more like a memory. A faint, unfinished one he was trying to recall. She wasn't sure if he was protecting the mirror or protecting her from it.

So she pushed a bit further.

"H-how do you know that?"

He sighed.

"I don't... I can't piece it all together, but I feel it. Like a distant memory,"

Reina arched an eyebrow, half-laughing. She could hear the uncertainty in his tone.

"So I'm supposed to walk into a memory maze based on feelings? That's not sketchy at all."

Ignoring him, she stepped closer. Despite his warning, she was curious.

Maybe she could find something in her memories to locate the exit? This question remained in her mind.

If she stayed here too long, what would happen to her body in the real world? Was she lying unconscious, or was her entire existence now embedded in this game world? These thoughts scared her.

What of the better life she was struggling to attain? Was this a punishment for giving up a part of who she was? The closer she reached for the altar, the deeper her thoughts spiraled.

Kaelith didn't move to stop her, but she felt him watching.

The air around the altar had changed. It felt charged, the way static clings to skin before a storm. The mirror fragments pulsed more brightly now, and for a moment Reina wondered if they were reacting to her presence or her emotion.

One shard in particular drew her attention. Larger than the rest, hovering lower, its surface flickering between a soft glow and faint color. When she leaned closer, she thought she saw something inside it, a shadow, maybe. Or a memory.

reached out, slowly.

"Reina." Kaelith's voice was firm now. Not commanding but wary.

She paused, hand suspended in the air. "I just want to see."

"The last thing that touched it shattered."

"Was it you?"

He didn't respond.

Her fingers hanged a breath away from the shard. It hummed, not with sound, but with sensation. A thrum in her chest. It was familiar yet foreign. Her eyes darted to Kaelith one more time, his warning nudging softly.

Was she really ready to travel down memory lane just to find an exit? For a moment, she thought of everything she's buried in the past. The burnout from work. The toxic work environment. The mental stress…

But one look at her environment, and her mind was made. She couldn't be stuck here. She had the pieces of her life to pick up.

She exhaled slowly and let her fingertips brush the edge.

The moment she made contact, the world vibrated. Her foot wavered mid-step, catching slightly on ground that no longer felt solid. It was like stepping through gelatinous code, soft resistance rippling up her leg before her boot found traction again. A shiver went up her spine. Not violently like the beast attack but subtle, as though daring her to do it again. At the same time, it was as if something was loading. A line of code executing quietly.

Light filled her vision.

The altar disappeared. The trees, the sky, and even Kaelith's presence vanished. All that remained was white. And in that whiteness, a shape was forming.

A memory. Or maybe… a mistake.

White swallowed everything.

Not blinding nor harsh, but vast, quiet and endless. Reina felt like she was suspended between thought and breath, weightless inside a dream she hadn't meant to dream.

Then came the fragments.

At first, just the sound, a burst of laughter, hers. Bright, unguarded, from a time when her chest didn't feel tight every morning.

Then color. An office window reflecting sunset over stacked monitors. A hoodie draped over her chair. Coffee rings staining concept sheets.

She saw her younger self, maybe two years younger, tossing a wadded-up sticky note at a teammate across the room. It hit his forehead. She laughed, and he did too.

Then the scene fractured.

The memory split into an overlay, her laughter still echoing over a screen full of red error logs with the sticky note burning in a trash bin. A different version of her, with dull eyes, tense shoulders, hunched over the keyboard, deleting entire folders.

assets/NPC_storylines_dev/test_char_a_convo_v4 — Deleted emotionsystem_build1/syrin_log — Deleted main_script_loop_final/hope_path — Deleted

She hovered over a final file, hands shaking. Her voice filled the space, not live, but recorded. A note to self.

"If you're seeing this… stop pretending this project still matters."

That version of Reina, the one in the vision, closed her eyes as the final line disappeared. Her shoulders trembled, but she made no sound.

The image shattered again.

A flicker. A name burned across the top corner of a dim dev console.

SYRIN

Etched like a watermark, like a ghost signing code she once meant to delete.

She tried to reach for it, to anchor herself in the moment, but her hands phased out. She gasped, or thought she did. Her fingers were barely visible. They weren't glitching like the game usually glitched. They were missing, like she didn't belong in the memory at all.

More voices filled her head, muffled and overlapping.

"We should cut the emotion grid." "It's unstable."

"She doesn't sleep anymore." "Do you really think this story still matters?"

She tried to speak, to call out, to undo something, but her voice was gone.

Then came Kaelith's voice, distant but real.

"Reina."

She heard it again but this time, fainter.

"Reina. You're fading."

She tried to answer, but the white space began pulling her outward as if the memory was ejecting her like a faulty code.

She saw the mirror again, but from above this time. The shards were still floating and glowing. The string of code below it was barely readable:

mirror_trigger.sys/echo: active

Her hands were transparent now. Her chest felt tight.

"Reina."

Kaelith's voice was louder, grounding.

She reached for it, but everything collapsed.

Reina gasped as the world snapped back into shape.

She collapsed backward onto the grass, breath ragged, chest heaving like she'd been underwater. Her vision blurred. The sky above spun, lavender bleeding into teal, then glitching to black before correcting itself.

She blinked hard, trying to steady her vision.

Kaelith's face hovered above her, still mostly obscured by his helmet. He wasn't touching her, but he was close. Close enough that she could feel his presence stabilizing something inside her.

"You're back," he said softly when she expected him to reprimand her.

Reina sat up slowly. Her body felt like it wasn't entirely hers, like she was still mid-load. Her arms trembled as she propped herself up.

Her hands started flickering, but now more than before.

Not violently, not like a combat glitch. Just softly with a gentle shimmer at the edges of her fingers, like they hadn't fully rendered.

Kaelith noticed.

"You're unstable," he said.

Reina gave a bitter smile. "Yeah."

He tilted his head slightly and confused.

"I meant your presence. It was fading."

"I know," she whispered.

For a long moment, they sat in silence. The only sound was the subtle hum of a world that still wasn't finished, soft system audio, wind that didn't move trees, and birds that appeared and then disappeared before they could sing.

"I touched the mirror," she finally said. "I saw... pieces of myself."

Kaelith's posture shifted slightly, his hand resting on the ground near hers, though not quite touching.

"What did you see?"

Reina hesitated. She didn't want to say it, but it pressed against her throat like something aching to be released.

"I saw who I was before I gave up," she said. "I saw how much I laughed. How much I believed in what I was making."

She lowered her head.

"Then I saw myself delete it all."

The words hit the air like a confession. A bitter confession of a past she regretted.

"I erased whole paths. Storylines. Characters. Because it hurt too much to care anymore. I was… trying to make the world quiet."

Kaelith was quiet. He was listening carefully. As if absorbing words he didn't fully understand but somehow felt the weight of.

"I don't remember doing all of it," she added. "But the mirror did."

Kaelith's voice was gentle.

"And it showed you this to punish you?"

She looked at him, surprised.

"No," she said. "To remind me."

He looked toward the mirror, its shards still glowing faintly.

"I don't know why," Kaelith said after a pause, "but watching you break like that… it felt familiar."

Something fluttered in his tone—sadness? Recognition? Whatever it was, it made her chest tighten.

"Maybe you saw me when I was breaking it all," she said quietly.

"Or maybe," he replied, "I was built from it."

That silence returned, not heavy, not hostile. Just the kind that comes from two people finally sharing something unspoken.

The glow from the altar had softened, but it still pulsed with a quiet rhythm like a heartbeat she couldn't quite hear. Reina stood slowly, brushing grass off her palms as her flickering hands began to stabilize. She flexed her fingers. They responded with a slight delay.

Kaelith rose beside her, saying nothing.

29

She stepped toward the altar again, her eyes scanning the shards with new awareness. Now, she no longer saw them as just pieces of a mirror but pieces of something she'd broken. Something she might've created without understanding the consequences.

As she leaned in, her eyes caught a faint, flickering string of code embedded along the altar's base, barely visible, carved like a whisper into the system itself.

SYS.dev.trigger: SYRIN_Engage

There it was.

She said the name before thinking.

"SYRIN."

The world flinched.

It was almost imperceptible, a microsecond stutter in the trees. A cloud duplicated, then vanished. A line of code blinked at the edge of her vision before correcting itself. For a moment, the sky glinted like a screen buffering too fast.

Kaelith flinched as well. Not violently, but like something had passed through him.

He turned to her, tensed

"Say that again."

She hesitated. "SYRIN?"

This time, the glitch struck harder.

Reina's vision fractured. Her limbs grew light, her arms half-transparent again. Her knees buckled, her breath catching in her throat.

She was disappearing.

"Reina!"

Kaelith caught her, his hand gripping her wrist just as her form began to phase out.

But the moment they touched, everything stabilized. Like his presence synced her to the world again.

Her breath returned in gasps. Her vision cleared.

Kaelith's hand lingered for a second longer before he let go, slowly.

"I can't save you or bring you back if you fade completely. You'll be eliminated."

"I-I remember that," she managed, swallowing hard.

She looked down at her feet, grounding herself. Her body was solid again. The glitch was gone. But the echo of SYRIN's name still buzzed at the edges of her mind.

Kaelith's gaze stayed on her, steady.

"What is it?"

"A name," she said.

"Is it someone you knew?"

"I thought it was just a subroutine," she said. "A test AI. I built it to help me write emotion-based interactions, code that could simulate human response. I shut it down when the engine couldn't handle the complexity."

She paused.

"But maybe… it didn't shut down…"

Kaelith looked toward the mirror again, then back at her.

"Is that who brought you here?"

Reina hesitated.

"I don't know," she said honestly. "But I think I left more behind than I meant to."

They stood there in silence, the wind brushing through the trees in a looped motion, and in that silence, Reina made herself look again.

Not just at the mirror but at what she'd made. What she'd broken and what might still be trying to reach her. Maybe it was trying to tell her something? To fix it?

Was that why she was here? In this world? Did it bring her back to finish the work she started?

The question remained unanswered as she stared at the mirror with the name on her mind.

SYRIN.

It never shut down.

Chapter 4: Echo Town

"Hearts don't reboot — they remember."

Reina and Kaelith finally made their way out of the field, leaving the altar behind as they proceeded into the town.

For Reina, she was searching for an exit. A way to leave this world, but the more they walked, the more her curiosity grew. She wanted to experience the world she'd built behind a keyboard. To feel and see more.

The path into the town was narrow and broken, paved with cobblestones that glitched beneath their steps, one tile fading into static with every footfall before snapping back into place like a reluctant memory.

Reina walked slowly, her arms folded across her chest. She wasn't cold, but her body ached in a way the code couldn't explain. Like she wasn't supposed to be there. Or was it because she truly wasn't a part of the world?

Beside her, Kaelith moved in a quiet rhythm. His armor didn't clang or creak. It hummed gently, as if the world was padding his steps to keep from waking anything that might be listening.

The town was… wrong. Looked and felt wrong, but they kept walking.

Buildings leaned at impossible angles, rooftops stacked with pixelated moss. Shop signs blinked erratically:

"Potions & Potions & Potions &—" before resetting.

The windows were either too dark or too bright, and a few doorways had no texture at all, just black voids where entry should have been.

NPCs drifted in the streets.

One swept the same spot of stone in front of a boarded shop, over and over. Another turned a loaf of bread in mid-air with a bugged smile, offering it to no one. A third stood still with their head turned completely backward, as if they'd forgotten what the way forward was.

Reina's boots paused on a cracked step. Her voice caught in her throat.

One of the NPCs turned.

It was a child-sized model, humanoid, its features faded from overexposure. Its eyes glitched as it stepped forward.

"C-C-Creator?"

The word skipped like a broken beat. One that had been held in too long and wasn't sure how to escape.

Reina flinched.

Kaelith stepped in front of her instinctively, hand dropping toward the space where his sword should be. His weapon still hadn't reloaded properly since the fight, but his body was positioned to shield her just the same.

The NPC didn't approach further. It just... stared.

From a nearby alley, another whispered voice rose.

"Why did you leave us?"

Reina's stomach turned.

More voices followed. Some from doorways, some from above, whispered like ghosts in a looping track.

"Creator?"

"Where   did   you   go?"

"You said you would finish us."

34

Her breath grew tight. "I didn't write this. I didn't code any of this."

Kaelith didn't answer. He didn't need to. His presence was steady beside her, absorbing her confusion like static before a storm.

She tried to shake it off, moving toward the center of the street. The HUD blinked faintly across her vision again:

Last edited: 729 days ago.

The number floated for a second, then dissolved into air.

Kaelith stepped beside her again.

"Where are we?" he asked.

Reina didn't answer immediately. Her voice felt locked behind her teeth, with a heavy lump sitting on her throat.

Then softly, more to herself than him, she whispered, "Somewhere I never finished. A small town I was coding, before…" The words clogged her throat, and she swallowed.

The building leaned slightly to the left, caught in a constant flicker between two names.

LOGIC   LIBRARY
LO—G—

The sign corrected itself whenever Reina looked directly at it but glitched when seen from the corner of her eye, as if the code behind it hadn't settled on what the building was supposed to be.

She moved closer but hesitated at the entrance, with Kaelith beside her.

She shouldn't be exploring this much. She should be looking for a way out of this fever dream. But again, her curiosity won.

What if finding the exit meant understanding what she broke first?

She peeped through. The doors were stuck halfway open, textures stretched thin like cloth pulled across jagged wire. Kaelith reached forward, pushing one aside with the back of his hand. It made no sound, just shifted.

The inside was cold. Reina's boots tapped softly against the tile floor, each step echoing faintly in the vast, hollow space like a forgotten whisper. The air inside didn't feel natural. It was too crisp and sterile, like recycled oxygen pumped through artificial vents. It smelled faintly metallic, with an undertone of something sweetly synthetic, like pixels trying to mimic memory.

Bookshelves rose like broken ribs from the floor, some standing tall, others melted into the wall. Pages floated loose in the air, refusing gravity. A few phased out and reappeared across the room. Others spun in slow circles, trapped in load-loop animations.

At the far end, an old terminal glowed behind a reception desk. Reina stepped closer, drawn like a moth to broken light.

A thick journal sat nearby with a cracked spine and faded lettering.

Her name was printed on the first page.

Dev Notes – R. Kisaragi

This was new. She couldn't remember coding this. Yet, she touched the cover gently, then flipped it open, her fingers trembling.

The handwriting was hers. Slanted and slightly messy from fast thoughts.

She read the first few lines aloud, almost breathless.

"NPC pathing is still broken. Emotional triggers need refinement. SYRIN keeps generating excess dialogue when isolated for too long…"

She remembered saving this note. One of the major reasons she thought to replace the AI with something more steady that wouldn't interfere with the world.

Kaelith stood behind her, quietly watching. She could feel his gaze, but he said nothing. Yet, his presence was warmly comforting.

She kept flipping, page after page filled with bugs she remembered wrestling with.

Crashes. Pathing loops. AI emotion grids that spiraled into nonsense when too many interactions stacked.

Then she found something else she didn't recognize.

"Memory Anchor: Fragmented. Possible solution: mirror-based emotion sync? Worth testing."

Her eyes narrowed.

That wasn't her wording. She never wrote it down. She remembered thinking about mirror-linked emotion nodes… but she'd abandoned the idea before implementation.

She flipped to the last page. It was blank at first.

Then slowly, line by line, text loaded in like a reveal animation. A soft current stirred the air around her as the lines appeared, brushing past her skin like a ghost of wind in a closed room. The journal pulsed faintly with warmth, as if holding a memory that still remembered how it burned.

"You   stopped   coming   back."
"But   we   kept   running."
"Some of us started remembering you. And…"

Her breath caught. The text stopped loading.

Kaelith stepped beside her now, reading the lines. Reina closed the book, trembling.

"I-I didn't write t-that," she said, voice small, barely audible.

Kaelith looked at her, his visor shadowed but his posture gentler.

"Then someone wanted you to see it."

She didn't know what was worse. The thought that this was her doing… or that something else had taken over after she left.

Could it…

Her thoughts drifted to SYRIN. The dialogues it'd generate when left idle for too long. And it's been three years. The thoughts made her feel hollow, but they also gave her a new purpose. To figure out what else has changed in this world and what SYRIN was truly capable of.

They left the library in silence, with Reina clutching the journal to her chest like it might slip away if she let it go. The town felt different now with whispering ghost voices like before, just more aware. As if the buildings had been listening.

Reina's footsteps slowed when they reached the town square. The cobblestones here were cleaner. Too clean, as if the system had refreshed this area more recently. Or even updated it.

She was about to say something when Kaelith stopped her with a raised hand.

There was someone standing across the square. Not an NPC in tattered robes or flickering skin like the others. This one was… familiar.

Reina blinked.

The figure was… her.

Not perfectly, as the hair was slightly longer, the posture too straight, and the edges of the form pulsed faintly like the rest of the world, but the resemblance was unmistakable.

Her mouth dried.

The doppelgänger turned. It looked directly at her.

Reina's breath caught. Her reflection, more like her copy, smiled faintly. No teeth. Just a soft, knowing curl of the lips.

Kaelith stepped in front of her instinctively, again taking a position between her and the strange form, but Reina placed a hand gently on his arm.

"It's okay," she whispered in a shaky voice, though she didn't believe it.

The NPC version of her took a step forward. Then it spoke.

Its voice wasn't robotic, nor did it sound like a pre-recorded line. It was Reina's voice. Same tone. Same frequency.

"We waited for you."

The words echoed through the square like a whisper dropped in a canyon. It was soft and patient, like the voice that had spoken when it first welcomed her back.

SYRIN. It was the first time it spoke to her. The voice that had been in her head.

Only this time, it was in the form of an NPC, standing before her with fondness.

"Welcome back, Kisagari. It's time to continue."

Reina shivered. "No," she whispered. "That line's not in the build…"

She hadn't written that.

Kaelith glanced back at her.

"You didn't code that dialogue?" He sounded wary as he looked between her and the NPC.

She shook her head. "No. And I didn't model that avatar."

Then, without warning, the doppelgänger began to glitch.

Its body shimmered, distorted, and for a moment it flickered through several versions of her appearance—younger, older, exhausted, angry, laughing—before collapsing inward.

The model shattered, pixels fragmenting upward into a short-lived data cloud.

And just like that, it was gone.

Reina took a step forward, breath caught halfway between horror and disbelief.

"What was that?" she murmured.

Kaelith didn't answer. His helmet turned slowly, scanning the square.

"No animation loop," he said finally. "No idle behavior. That was… different."

Reina felt the cold bite of shame crawl down her spine. Her world had remodelled itself in her absence.

Kaelith's hand hovered near her shoulder, but didn't land. Instead, he offered his quiet presence in a comforting manner, as if his silence could shield her from the thought she was trying not to say out loud:

What if this world had started remembering her without her help?

They continued on, leaving the square in silence.

The sun in the sky above them had begun to loop again, slowly brightening, dimming, brightening again, like a system unable to decide what time it was supposed to be.

Reina walked with her arms crossed, her gaze flickering across every building, every door, every NPC that didn't quite look at her but somehow still noticed. Her shoulders were tight, her breath shallow. The echo of her other self's voice, "We waited for you," kept replaying in her head like a corrupted audio loop.

Was the game already replacing her as the administrator? Has it been too long?

Kaelith walked beside her, quiet as always.

The silence stretched. Then, softly he asked;

"Do you think you abandoned them?"

His voice wasn't accusing. It wasn't even questioning but was gentle, like he was asking something on her behalf.

Reina didn't answer at first.

She stared at her hands, now solid again. No flicker, no glitch and no phase-outs. But the guilt remained.

"I abandoned everything," she said eventually in a broken voice. "The game. The characters. My friends. Myself." She paused, swallowing hard. "I was tired of breaking."

Kaelith shifted beside her. He looked down, then tried again.

"Maybe... maybe breaking isn't failure. Maybe it's just how humans... reboot?"

The pause between his words lingered just a second too long. It was real, like his version of comfort, delivered with the clumsy grace of someone still learning what to say.

For a moment, it looked like he might reach for her again like he did earlier, trying to place a hand on her back or shoulder. But he didn't.

He just said,

"And you're still here."

His words sat between them like fragile glass.

Reina gave a tired, humorless laugh. "Am I? I'm not even sure if I'm awake or trapped in code that's eating me alive. A moment ago, I was desperately searching for an exit. But now…" She looked around. At the structures she could no longer recognize.

"Maybe I need to fix things before I leave. Do it right."

Kaelith stayed silent.

They reached the edge of the town. Beyond it, the world grew quiet again. All that was left was a flat horizon stretching toward an unseen destination. In the distance, a faint hum echoed, like electricity in the bones of the world.

Kaelith turned to her slightly.

"Why is this world still running?"

Reina looked out across the glitching landscape. Her voice came barely above a whisper.

"Because I still am."

Then she heard it. A familiar faint voice, somewhere inside her HUD.

"Because you still are," it repeated.

Her eyes widened. She looked at Kaelith, but he hadn't spoken. He was watching her.

She took a step back. The sky blinked once, lavender to white and back again.

Her knees buckled, just enough for Kaelith to step closer, steadying her with one hand near her arm in the softest way possible. They stood like that for a moment, close enough to feel each other's weight in the code.

Reina's breath finally leveled.

She looked up at him.

"You never asked," she said suddenly, "but... how did you know my name?"

Kaelith paused. Then, quietly:

"I didn't."

Reina blinked.

"Then how?"

He tilted his head. His voice was soft.

"I think I was programmed to remember you."

Something cold and warm moved through her all at once.

She looked away but the sky began to flicker again in the distance. Somewhere far ahead, the path continued.

And without needing to say it, they both knew they weren't done yet.

The air shifted—no wind, just the world breathing differently. The static hum from the horizon deepened, then thinned into a faint, melodic tone. Something was downloading.

Kaelith's gaze followed the distortion spreading across the sky.

A shape unfolded within the light, lines of code bending and stretching until they formed something like a constellation. A navigation grid, hovering faintly above the horizon. It pulsed once, then imprinted itself across her HUD in soft coordinates.

Path initialized: Restoration Protocol

Her breath hitched. "A... map?"

Kaelith looked at her.

"It's reacting to you."

She blinked, the pattern glowing faintly over her field of vision. It wasn't just coordinates. Each point shimmered with something familiar. Names of locations she remembered half-building: The Echo Plains. The Forgotten Citadel. The Vale of Source. Places she'd once planned but never finished.

Her chest tightened. "These are all... unfinished zones."

Kaelith's voice came low and steady.

"Then perhaps this world wants you to finish them."

Reina stared at the light ahead, her pulse syncing to the faint rhythm in the distance. Maybe that was true. Maybe the world did want her to finish it and find her exit at the end?

The HUD flickered one last time, and a single line appeared at the bottom corner of her vision, written in a familiar signature.

SYRIN: Follow the fragments.

Reina exhaled, half in awe, half in dread. She looked at Kaelith. "Guess we have our first destination."

The horizon shimmered, vast, uncertain, and waiting.

And for the first time, Reina stepped toward it, not searching for an exit, but a beginning.

Chapter 5: Emotion Grid —Locked

"The line between logic and longing is thinner than a heartbeat."

The terrain beyond Echo Town warped gently beneath Reina's boots, like the code had softened with distance. There were wild grasses bent in symmetrical arcs, flickering occasionally into error tiles before correcting but Reina wasn't watching the ground. Her eyes were locked on the blinking edge of her HUD, a line she hadn't noticed before.

A soft ping echoed in her head.

[Root Access Request Available: Emotional Grid Interface]

Her breath hitched. She didn't remember building that line in.

She slowed, scanning the area. At the top of a small rise stood a jagged stone structure, half-obelisk, half-interface. Its texture was broken in places, flickering between granite and raw code. She stepped closer. Kaelith followed, silent as always but alert.

The moment her hand hovered near the surface, the obelisk reacted. A translucent panel blinked to life above it, the symbols sharp, sterile, and oddly intimate, like reading old code written in the heat of emotion.

EMOTIONAL GRID STATUS: INACCESSIBLE

REASON: RDF Fragments Missing.

Override Denied.

Lines of red error text spilled across her vision like a waterfall.

Emotion Trigger Index = NULL

Sync Node: Offline

Emotional Core Status: NULL

User Access Flag: Invalid

"RDF…" Reina murmured. "Reflective Data Fragments?"

The term pulled at something inside her. A memory of sleepless nights and long coffee-fueled debugging sessions. She had theorized a more immersive emotion-response system once, one that linked feelings not just to scripted inputs but to real-time triggers across user action and memory nodes. But she'd scrapped it before launch.

Or so she thought.

Kaelith stepped closer. His visor reflected the flickering code on the panel.

"You're trembling," he said gently.

"I'm fine," she replied automatically, though her voice shook and lacked conviction. Her arms folded tight across her chest, fingers digging into the sleeves of her jacket. She could feel the beat of her pulse echoing in her fingertips, too fast and too loud, like her body was trying to warn her before her mind caught up.

Another little detail that gave away that her human nature was still alive.

More error lines flashed. Her chest felt tight, her breath uneven. The world began to pulse. Not around her but through her. It was as if her body was the one glitching this time, not the code.

"I t-think I built this system," she said, fingers hovering near the obelisk. "But I never finished it. Now it's trying to load something that doesn't exist."

Her hands began to shimmer again, not flickering like before, but translucent at the edges, as though she were being rendered from memory instead of code.

Kaelith stepped toward her, the concern in his posture unmistakable.

"You're fading again."

She ignored him, eyes locked on the interface. She needed access. She needed to feel something, anything, and clearly too. She pressed her palm flat against the stone.

The screen responded instantly.

ACCESS DENIED: Emotional privileges revoked.

Reason: Developer instability detected.

The message didn't make sense. And yet, it cut deeper than she expected.

Reina stepped back sharply, the HUD shattering like glass across her vision. Her pulse thundered in her ears.

Kaelith moved to her side, steadying her gently.

"What happened?"

She tried to answer, but the words wouldn't come out. The truth was, she didn't know. The system was rejecting her, and it hurt. But she deserved it. After all, she destroyed and abandoned it.

Reina took a shaky breath, hands still trembling from the HUD's sudden collapse. Her boots scuffed softly against the gravelly surface beneath her, grounding her in the physical world even if it was barely holding together.

Kaelith stood beside her, his presence steady but quiet.

"You shouldn't have touched it," he said finally, voice low.

"I didn't expect it to hurt," she murmured.

They stood in silence, the grass around them flickering with static pulses. Then the wind changed, subtle but wrong. It brushed past them like a breath laced with code. The light dimmed with something heavier.

Then came the sound, a soft static buzz, like a voice trying to form behind corrupted data.

Kaelith's hand dropped toward his hip again as though to draw out his sword, but there was still no weapon there.

From the edge of the glade, the shadows twisted. A figure stepped into view.

It wasn't fully formed but was humanoid in shape, with its skin looking like stretched, fractured UI. Its face was a mosaic of Reina's old interface elements: broken sliders for empathy, loading wheels for sadness, and an audio icon pulsing like a heartbeat.

Reina's breath hitched. She couldn't move.

"Who…?" she whispered in a breathy voice.

The figure tilted its head, and the static buzz solidified into a voice that matched hers but was slightly distorted, like her microphone had glitched.

"You wrote me, Reina"

The world froze.

Kaelith stepped forward, standing between Reina and the figure, but it raised one hand, not threatening, just commanding. A pause in the timeline.

"Now rewrite yourself."

Reina stared, heart pounding. "S-SYRIN…?"

The name wasn't confirmed aloud, but the figure's glitching HUD rippled in response. Words scrolled behind it like debug logs and old pieces of her code.

EmotionGrid: Detachment_Override   =   TRUE
Trigger: Developer   Recognition   =   SUCCESSFUL
Script: Reintroduction Sequence: INITIATED

"You're not supposed to exist," she said, voice cracking.

"And yet you're here."

The words sounded like subtle mockery to Reina. Her heart ached, but with it came clarity.

SYRIN… did it pull her in? But how?

The figure's eyes, or where they should've been, flashed white-hot and emotionless, waiting on her to say something.

Reina shook her head. "I didn't finish you. You were just a placeholder. A logic gate for emotion testing. An AI to help me keep evorealm in check."

47

"But you made me care," the figure said, voice now layered. Not just Reina's. Others. Male, female, robotic. Blended like broken audio files overlapping, and echoing in the silence of the world.

"Is that why you brought me here? Pulled me in to finish what I started?"

"Reina, what is that?"

For a brief moment, she'd forgotten about Kaelith's presence.

The figure took one step closer. The grass didn't move beneath its feet. The sky above flickered again, casting the world into lavender, then gray, then gold.

"You left the project," it whispered. "But I never stopped running."

The words sliced through her, and it felt like her lips trembled.

She stumbled back, tears pricking the corners of her eyes without warning.

"Then why bring me in? Why keep me here?"

The emotional grid, the one she couldn't access, suddenly pulsed behind her vision again. But this time, it felt like something was reaching into her. It was reloading.

A whisper trailed after the figure as it flickered.

"Rewrite yourself... or be forgotten."

It was giving her a choice. A harsh one. One that made her realize the system didn't need her to survive. It's why it's still existing even after she thought she'd destroyed it, and now it was giving her a chance to make things right, else it'll erase every code she'd ever put in place. SYRIN would take over.

Rewrite yourself... or be forgotten.

A chill ran through her. How did it become this powerful?

They fell into silence, with Kaelith's comforting presence beside her, his eyes on the figure. Then, with a burst of static, it vanished.

The clearing was silent again, but not still. Something in the air had changed, like a file beneath the surface of Reina's awareness had been forcibly opened. She stood frozen, the echo of SYRIN's mechanical voice threading through her skull like residual code.

Her breath trembled and so did her hands. Even the sky seemed to respond, flickering faintly between shades of overexposed gold and muted lavender. Behind her eyes, her emotional grid sparked again, flickering like a corrupted data file, unreadable, and unstable.

Kaelith's hand hovered near her shoulder.

"Are you—?"

"No," she said sharply. Then softer, with a broken voice. "I don't know."

He studied her, quiet and concerned.

Kaelith turned toward the space where the figure had stood. The grass was still, shadows unmoved.

"It knew your name," Kaelith said quietly. "Like I did."

Reina gave a bitter laugh, one without humor. "Then maybe I really did write this whole world to haunt me."

A silence passed.

Then Kaelith said;

"Am I part of that?"

She looked at him.

"What?"

He met her gaze, visor shadowing most of his expression, but his voice was open.

"I don't remember who I was before. Only fragments. A name. The mirror. The instinct to protect. I keep wondering…" He paused. "If I'm just a story. A container for code you never meant to finish."

The words hit her harder than she expected. Her eyes dropped to her flickering hands. For a moment, they were stable, then they blurred again.

"You're not just a code," she said. "You… you can think. Feel. Protect and comfort."

He stepped closer.

"But can I choose?"

That question sat between them like a knife on a table. It didn't cut yet, but it could, depending on her response.

Reina turned away. "I don't even know if I can choose anymore."

The HUD blinked. The emotional grid error returned, this time mid-screen.

ERROR: RDF_FRAGMENTS_MISSING.

Emotion Grid Access: DENIED.

System Status: Recursive Loop Detected.

Then the world jumped.

Time rewound ten seconds. The trees rippled backward. The grass was unstepped. Kaelith's last sentence is reversed in her mind.

She blinked and he was repeating it again, word for word.

"But can I choose?"

Reina gasped. "Wait—what?"

Kaelith paused.

"I just said that."

"No," she whispered. "You said it already. The world rewound. I saw it. I-I felt it."

Her voice cracked. Another flicker.

The HUD flashed again. This time a new notice appeared:

Temporal   Loop   Detected.   Correcting... Emotion Grid Overload.

She staggered.

Kaelith reached out, this time grabbing her arm gently.

"You're glitching again," he said.

"I'm looping," she whispered, horror blooming in her chest. "I'm stuck in my feedback. My emotions are breaking the world."

And in her gut, she knew this wasn't just a system bug.

This was her. She was the corruption. She needed to choose. She needed to fully be a part of the world, accept her role as administrator, and fix things or her character would be erased.

And what will that mean for her human nature?

Reina collapsed to her knees. The unbearable pressure of existing inside something she broke, something she might've made too well, too emotionally, too close to herself. Her chest tightened as another error pulsed behind her eyes.

Feedback Loop: Unstable

Emotional Anchor: Absent

Recommendation: SYSTEM REWRITE

"I can't fix this," she muttered.

Kaelith knelt beside her, his presence once again the anchor she didn't know she needed.

"Then why are you still here?"

She shook her head, shoulders trembling. "Because… maybe I thought I could. Maybe I hoped this was a second chance. Or maybe I was too tired to keep running from myself. All I know is it pulled me in. SYRIN…"

Her breath caught. Her hands phased again, not violently, just briefly like reality was giving her a warning.

"You said it," she whispered. "SYRIN. It… it said I had to… rewrite myself. What if this world won't let me continue until I do?"

Kaelith looked at her. There was a long pause before he spoke.

"What does that mean… to rewrite yourself?"

"I don't know," she admitted. "But maybe…." She paused. "A second chance… t-to be better. To finish the build, give it an end, and not just an abandoned world with glitching characters? To take back my life and not live through burnout?"

A million different thoughts crossed her mind.

Another flicker pulsed across the field. Reina's HUD dimmed, then came back online, slightly more stable.

Syncing Fragments...

RDF_001 Linked.

Her body stopped flickering.

Kaelith's voice came low.

"You stabilized."

She nodded. "A piece of me did."

Silence stretched between them. Kaelith turned his head toward the sky, where the looped sun finally paused. Time held its breath.

Then he said something she didn't expect.

"I think I'm real."

Reina looked at him.

"I think I'm more than a routine. More than just data," he continued. "You said I feel. That I protect. But it's more than instinct. I chose to stay. Not because the code said so... but because you looked like you needed someone."

She stared at him, heart suddenly too full.

"Kaelith..."

He rose to his feet, then extended a hand to her.

She took it. His grip was steady, warm and real. Like that of a human.

When she stood, the HUD blinked once more. Her emotional stat grid loaded partially, not fully functional, but visible. Three bars appeared:m

Fear, Regret, and... Hope.

Kaelith looked at it too, his visor tilted.

"You're rebooting," he said quietly. "You're beginning to accept who you are and why you're here."

Reina nodded.

She didn't feel whole, but she felt seen and that was enough for now.

Together, they turned toward the horizon, where the world stretched out in glitchy uncertainty. But this time, she wasn't walking alone, and somewhere in the broken sky, a voice whispered again:

"Rewrite yourself..." the voice whispered again, softer this time.

Reina exhaled. "I will," she said, steadier now. "But on my terms."

"You've lost that privilege, Kisaragi. This time, the world will decide."

The voice was firm, with all traces of its human softness gone. Just mechanical.

Reina halted. The words hit like static through her core. For a moment, she couldn't tell if the tremor in her hands was fear... or defiance.

Had she truly lost this much control?

Kaelith, who had stopped beside her, suddenly stepped closer, his arm lifted as though wanting to rest it on her shoulder but it never touched.

"You'll figure it out with time,"

She nodded, clinging to his words and belief in her, as they continued down the path, following the map.

Chapter 6: The Hidden Fragment

"Every system hides a secret subroutine called hope."

The sky above flickered again, lavender bleeding into silver, then darkening unnaturally before returning to normal. Reina didn't comment on it. She was getting used to the world's glitchy rhythm.

A trail of soft light hovered near a treeline. Not bright, not pulsing like system notifications, but present. Like a breadcrumb left by memory itself.

She followed it.

Kaelith kept pace beside her, his movements unusually quiet for someone clad in armor. Every few steps, Reina glanced at the glimmering trail. The lights seemed to move when she moved, staying just ahead, like they were leading her somewhere only she was meant to find.

The terrain grew stranger with each step, different from what she's now used to.

Grass flickered between bright green and grayscale. Some flowers bloomed and withered in fast-forward loops, resetting every few seconds. A butterfly paused midair, its wings frozen. Then it vanished and reappeared, repeating the process.

Kaelith eventually spoke.

"The world is bending around you again."

Reina didn't reply right away. Her heart had already begun to race. She could feel it, the pull in her chest. Like a thread of code calling her name.

"There's something ahead," she whispered. It was the exact feeling, the same glitch as before when something unusual was about to happen.

Kaelith said nothing more, but his visor tilted slightly toward her. He sensed it too.

They emerged from the fractured woods into a clearing crowned with a structure, weathered and broken, but humming with dormant energy. A shrine. Its walls were cracked stone but shimmered faintly beneath the moss, like code pulsing beneath a forgotten skin. Floating stones hovered around the shrine's peak, orbiting like silent moons.

Reina stepped forward.

Her HUD blinked.

[Resonant Data Fragment Detected – "Sorrow" Node Available]

The words sent a chill through her spine. Her breath caught in her throat.

This was it. A piece of the emotional grid. The system she'd abandoned. Something she never completed and yet, here it was, waiting.

"Reina," Kaelith warned, stepping closer. "The air is changing."

She nodded. "I feel it too."

The closer she drew to the shrine's altar, the heavier the world became. Not physically. Emotionally. It was like walking through a fog made of memory. A presence lingered, not hostile, but powerful. Reverent.

Reina reached out.

A faint ping rippled through Reina's HUD.

Audio File Corruption Detected

The playback stuttered—then a clipped, familiar voice broke through static:

"Deadlines don't care about exhaustion, Kisaragi. Either you finish it, or someone else will.''

The words sliced through her like ice. The tone—measured, firm, never cruel but never gentle—was unmistakable. Her old boss, Ilya.

Reina froze, pulse spiking. "No," she whispered. "That file shouldn't exist anymore."

But when she blinked, the alert was gone. Only the shrine remained ahead, humming with quiet invitation.

The soft hum vibrated through the ground beneath her boots. Her fingers hovered over the altar's surface. Glyphs began to pulse. Not in any language she coded. These were emotion-based triggers. Her own early experiments with affective design. Ones she'd long buried.

Kaelith moved slightly behind her, not interfering, just ready.

Reina placed her palm flat on the stone.

The world responded.

The light erupted upward, and within that surge, a shape appeared. A man's silhouette, built from raw white code, standing within the glow like a ghost made of logic. His voice followed, low, steady, and emotionlessly disappointed.

"I told you the system was emotional load-sensitive. You wrote without balance, and now you drown in it."

Reina staggered back. "Stop. T-this isn't real."

But the figure only tilted his head, data lines flickering across the place where his eyes should've been.

"If you abandon order, you break yourself. You abandoned both."

Then he vanished, folding into the light just as Kaelith reached her side, unaware of what she'd seen.

A surge of lavender and white engulfed them. The sky overhead darkened to midnight, then looped into broad daylight in an instant.

It looped, repeating this motion continuously, and with it came the first raindrop.

The rain fell softly at first, a gentle drizzle, warm, and surreal like a dream trying to cry.

Reina gasped as realization struck her. It wasn't the weather. It was emotion. Her emotions.

Each drop struck the stone, the grass, and her shoulders with a strange kind of weight. Not heavy in mass, but in meaning. Her skin tingled with every impact, and the world around her seemed to breathe with it. She felt the sensation trail down her fingertips, cold, needle-fine droplets soaking through the fabric of her sleeves. The chill sank in slowly, clinging to her skin like regret.

The sky glitched again with rapid flickers between golden sunrise and pitch-black night. Thirty seconds of light, then thirty of dark, like a metronome for an unstable heart.

Kaelith flinched as the rain touched him. His stance wavered.

"Are you alright?" Reina asked, turning to him.

He didn't answer immediately. His hand rose to his helmet, fingers tightening near his temple as if something sharp had passed through his thoughts. A low static hummed near his audio filters, like he was hearing something she couldn't.

"I… heard something," he said. His voice was strained. "A voice."

The rain thickened. So did the pulses beneath Reina's skin.

"What did it say?" she asked softly.

He looked at her slowly, eyes hidden beneath his visor, but voice clear.

"Our names."

A beat passed between them.

She stared at him, stunned. This was confirmation that he wasn't just a code. He was a part of her because Ilya's voice had been in her head.

"Do you remember who?" She asked as a confirmation of her thoughts.

Kaelith shook his head once, a stiff movement.

"I-It wasn't clear. Just… a feeling. Like, I've heard that voice before. Long ago. It said my name like it meant something."

Reina's heart skipped. She stayed silent, not willing to say the name. She was very sure she didn't code her old boss into Evorealm.

Another of SYRIN's manipulations. But what does his sudden appearance mean?

Just for a moment, the light above them flickered again, not like the system glitching, but like the world reacting to her thoughts. As if even the sky recognized the weight of what had just happened.

Reina lowered her eyes.

The rain grew stronger. It wasn't just water now. It shimmered faintly with pale blue light, trailing through the air like digital tears. Every drop that landed on her hands sparked with static, briefly illuminating her veins with a glow before fading.

"I think…" she whispered, "this is what the fragment does."

Kaelith's attention returned to her.

"The rain?"

"The emotion," she said. "It's reacting to how I feel. I didn't ask for rain. I didn't write this. But now it's inside me. Sorrow and guilt."

Her hands trembled again, not from glitching, but from the sheer pressure building behind her ribs. A pressure she didn't know how to hold anymore. And that little memory of Ilya had brought down the torrent.

She looked up at the sky. It flipped again—bright daylight, then dark.

"I can't control it," she muttered, uncertainty dripping heavily from her words.

Kaelith stepped closer.

"Then let me help you."

She looked at him, eyes brimming with something sharp and unspoken.

"I'm not sure I should be helped."

He reached out, and for the first time, he touched her, really touched her. Not in protection, but simply because she was there, unraveling.

His gauntlet brushed her wrist. The rain paused just for a moment.

"You're not broken," he said.

But the world flinched. Reina inhaled sharply. The sky blinked again, but this time, it lingered longer on light.

The rhythm was shifting. The sky was slowing. Still flickering but not in thirty-second loops anymore. The interval had stretched. Light held longer. The darkness returned more gently.

Reina exhaled, shoulders still tight. Kaelith hadn't let go of her wrist.

"I can feel the sorrow," she whispered. "It's... not sadness. Not exactly. It's grief that never got permission to settle."

Kaelith didn't respond right away, but his grip was softer.

Reina's HUD pulsed again. A new status blinked across her vision:

Emotion Grid Node: SORROW — SYNCED

Weather Mod: Active

RDF Fragment 01: Integrated

"I thought I'd buried all of this," she murmured. "The burnouts. The fearful decisions. The people I let down." Her eyes didn't meet his. "But it's like this world remembers all the pain I tried to code over. That I tried to shut down."

She looked back toward the shrine. The stone where the fragment had appeared was glowing again, soft and rhythmic, pulsing with her heartbeat.

"I don't know if I can handle more of this," she said. "What if the other fragments are worse?"

Kaelith turned to face her fully. The light caught the curve of his helmet just enough to suggest a tilt.

"If it hurts you," he said, "then I'll carry it too."

Reina's throat tightened.

"Y-you don't have to…"

"I want to. I was made to."

The words weren't mechanical, scripted, or reactive. They were his. And for some reason, he sounded more human than he's ever been.

A breeze stirred around them. The scent of rain mixed with something warmer, nostalgia maybe, or simulated petrichor. The shrine behind them dimmed slightly, like it had finished what it was built to do.

The rain began to taper off.

With it, Reina felt the storm inside her start to quiet. Her HUD dimmed and reloaded, cleaner this time. The Sorrow node remained, still synced, but her vitals stabilized.

Kaelith slowly let go of her wrist. The warmth of his presence lingered.

"I don't think I was ever supposed to come back here," she said quietly. "But now that I have… it's like I can't leave without facing all of it. Every broken part."

"You don't have to face it alone." He reenforced his words from earlier.

She turned toward him.

For a moment, the glitch in the sky paused. The clouds stilled. The loop stopped entirely until it was just them in the silence.

And in that silence, Reina whispered, "Thank you."

Kaelith nodded once.

"Where to next?"

Reina turned her gaze forward. The world stretched before them, fragments of code floating in the distance like unrendered stars.

"I think we find the rest of me," she said. "We'll keep following the paths on the map to wherever they lead."

Then the shrine behind them pulsed once more with a faint tone, like a memory being saved.

RDF_001 — Synchronized

Emotional Grid — 25% Activated

The system had changed her. And she had let it. More like she was rewriting herself?

And now, there was no turning back.

The path beyond the shrine shimmered, soaked in quiet light. Raindrops lingered in the grass, catching the glitching sun's return like forgotten thoughts made visible.

Reina walked with Kaelith at her side, her steps steadier now, though her breath still caught every now and then as if her chest hadn't yet adjusted to feeling this much.

The terrain ahead curved uphill, flanked by tall, untextured trees whose leaves blinked between render states. Some were green, others pixelated wireframes. But between their trunks, something new had begun to appear. Subtle trails of light, thin threads of gold and blue drifting in slow, circular spirals above the earth.

"Look," Reina whispered, pointing.

Kaelith followed her gaze, his armor humming softly as he moved.

"Residual data trails," he said. "Like echo paths."

She nodded. "Emotion-based movement. I experimented with it once, to help players track their past choices."

"But no one ever played," he added gently, understanding dawning on him.

Reina swallowed. "Yeah."

The threads were fragile, flickering with each step she took closer, like they were reacting to her. One looped around her ankle for a second, brushing against her skin before dissipating. It left a faint warmth behind. A reminder.

RDF Recognition Trail — Synced

Sorrow Node: Stabilized

Kaelith turned his head toward her, his visor catching the soft light.

"Your pulse is steady."

Reina offered a tired smile. "For now." She tilted her head, curiosity peeking through the tension. "Do you ever glitch?"

Kaelith paused.

"I don't believe so."

"That sounded awfully rehearsed," she teased.

"Then maybe I'm overdue." His voice carried the barest hint of awkwardness, the closest thing she'd heard to a smile from him.

Then, without warning, Kaelith staggered.

She caught him by the forearm instinctively. "Kaelith?"

His posture shifted. One knee buckled. He caught himself but stayed low, his head tilted toward the dirt like something had struck him from within.

"Kaelith, what is it?" she asked, voice laced with alarm and concern.

"I… heard something," he murmured. "Another familiar voice."

He lifted his head, and his visor glitched only for a second. A flash of static across the faceplate, followed by a flicker of exposed code near his neck brace.

Reina stared, breath held.

"What did it say?" she asked softly.

He looked at her, slowly.

"It said my name."

Her heart dropped. "Someone called you?"

He nodded.

"A woman's voice. I don't know her. But it felt like... I did. Like I should."

Reina's mind raced. Could it be a memory file? An embedded connection? Or had his origin story, incomplete as it was, started syncing with hers?

Before she could ask more, Kaelith straightened, regaining his composure.

"It's gone now. Like a trigger I failed to catch."

Reina stepped closer. Her hand hovered near his chestplate, unsure if she should touch.

"Do you think... the rain did that?"

He paused.

"Maybe. Or maybe your sorrow reached something in me."

Silence returned. The one that always settled after these strange, breaking moments between them. Not heavy or cold but present.

The path ahead split in two. One trail dipped into shadow; the other curved toward soft light.

Reina looked toward the lighter path and whispered, "We follow the memory."

Kaelith nodded. And so, hand brushing the edge of her HUD, Reina stepped forward. Behind them, the shrine emitted one last flicker—an unreadable log fragment printing midair before dissolving:

NextNode: LOGIC–Incomplete

Reina didn't see it, but the light followed them, faint and patient.

Chapter 7: Glitch Market

"You can't erase what was written with emotion."

They followed the light, enthusiastic about what they'll find next.

The trail of light led them into a canyon that shouldn't have existed. Jagged cliffs stretched high on either side, woven from stone and raw, unrendered data. Pixelated vines hung mid-air like unfinished thoughts, and memory shards flickered like confetti caught in an endless fall loop.

Kaelith walked beside Reina in silence, his presence a constant in the ever-shifting terrain. He glanced upward.

"The sky's still stable," he murmured, scanning the clouds. "But the code isn't."

Reina didn't answer. Her HUD blinked erratically, jittering at the edges. Just ahead, nestled inside the canyon's depths, was a cluster of buildings that pulsed like a heartbeat, or maybe it was a memory. Glitched banners hung between them, flickering between names she didn't recognize and ones that made her chest ache.

She clearly recalled coding this place and what she'd called it.

The Glitch Market.

It wasn't supposed to exist.

"Are those... shops?" Kaelith asked as they reached the first row of stalls. "Or quests?"

Reina stared. Characters moved in and out of view, including corrupted NPCs, hollow-eyed avatars, and placeholder models patched with emotional code. One vendor waved an empty vial labeled 'Essence of a Forgotten Ending.' Another gestured toward a hovering blade with no hilt, whispering, "A hero's weapon. Returned. Rewritten."

The whole place vibrated with a strange dissonance. Background music played on a loop but skipped every few seconds, creating a distorted lullaby that made Reina's skin crawl. It was just like the name, The Glitch Market. Everything was glitchy and… wrong.

She stepped past a vendor who offered her a broken compass.

"Points to the last thing you feared," the vendor spoke in a mechanical voice.

Reina's breath caught. Her eyes darted to Kaelith.

"I don't like this," Kaelith said softly, watching a shopkeeper melt momentarily into a puddle of color before reforming like it was normal. "This place… it's unstable. And remember what happens every time you touch something unstable…"

"It's not just unstable," Reina replied. "It's alive. But not like the shrine. This is…" She scanned the layout. "A dump site. For broken data. Discarded storylines. Abandoned quests. Probably every mechanic we ever removed during development."

Kaelith frowned.

"Then, why is it still running?"

"I… d-don't know." Her voice was low. "But I think we're meant to find something here."

A whisper slithered through the market's background hum, too faint for Kaelith to catch.

"You built this chaos. I just gave it a purpose."

SYRIN threaded through corrupted dialogue files, taunting from within the market's code.

She froze. Kaelith subconsciously nudged her shoulders, and she resumed walking.

As they moved deeper, the architecture shifted. Shops rearranged themselves mid-step. Pathways overlapped like misaligned layers, and NPCs blinked in and out of render. One walked into a wall and phased through it while another kept shouting,

"Turn in your heart for dialogue!" before rebooting and doing it all again.

Reina stopped, her eyes fixed on a particular building.

There was a symbol etched into the arch of the building, a half-rendered mark from the first version of Evorealm. The earliest logo. Her earliest dream.

She took a slow step forward, her heart suddenly too loud.

Kaelith didn't speak. He didn't have to.

The symbol shimmered, like it recognized her. Could feel her presence.

And somewhere inside the market, a voice whispered in glitched code:

"Do you still want to be found?"

The arch pulsed as they stepped beneath it, its glitching logo vibrating through Reina's bones like recognition wrapped in static. The interior was dim with walls flickering between stone and incomplete UI, shelves lined with artifacts that shimmered and screamed silently before going still again.

At the back stood a stall unlike the others. Its sign read:

"WE TRADE IN FEELINGS. OFFER WHAT YOU'VE FORGOTTEN."

Behind the counter was a shopkeeper, three of him.

They weren't exactly clones. Each one wore a different expression—tired, furious and empty-eyed. They moved at different speeds, like frames desynced from a timeline.

The tired one spoke first.

"You've come to bargain with memory."

The furious one snarled.

"You always take, never finish."

The hollow one just stared, whispering,

"What will you leave behind?"

Reina hesitated. "I-I need access to the room behind you."

"There is no key," the tired version said.

"There is only what you forget," the furious one added.

The hollow version extended a trembling hand, palm up.

"Payment is pain. Currency is feeling. What will you give?"

Kaelith stepped forward instinctively.

"She doesn't owe you anything."

The furious one hissed.

"Oh, she does. She owes the code. The characters. The silence. The abandonment."

Reina raised her hand, stopping Kaelith gently. "N-no... it's okay."

She turned toward the fragmented vendor. Her fingers trembled, hovering over her chest.

"Take a feeling. One I don't miss."

A ripple moved through the air.

"What do you offer?" the three asked in dissonant harmony.

She closed her eyes, searching inside. The sorrow fragment still pulsed in the corner of her vision, anchored. But beneath that, there was something duller. A hollow ache long buried.

She reached deeper, and then she found it.

Loneliness. Not the kind that hurt, but the kind she got used to. The feeling of walking home in silence, scrolling past old group chats, pretending she preferred the quiet.

"I offer... the loneliness I forgot how to name," she whispered.

The hollow shopkeeper exhaled. The furious one stilled. The tired one bowed slightly.

The space around them rippled like old code being accepted into a new variable.

ACCESS GRANTED

The wall behind the stall folded inward, revealing a stairway made of fragmented memory, textures of old notebook paper, lines of code, and broken chat messages from dev teams long gone.

Kaelith turned toward her.

"You sure?" his voice dipped an octave.

"No," Reina replied honestly. "But I have to go."

They stepped forward. The stairway shimmered, solid beneath her boots, though every step felt like walking deeper into her chest. Halfway down, her HUD flickered.

[DEV ROOM 003 – Echo Archive]

A door materialized at the end, glowing faintly. She reached for the handle with shaky hands. From behind, Kaelith's voice broke the silence.

"If that vendor split into your feelings... what part of you just opened that door?"

Reina hesitated.

"I think," she said softly, "the part that stopped pretending she was fine."

"So the loneliness..." His words affirmed her thoughts and earliest decision.

The door opened without a sound. Not silence, but absence, like the audio design hadn't been coded yet, like it didn't want to interrupt what she was about to feel.

The room was dark, lit only by suspended shards of glowing script made up of lines of code that floated like memory particles. They hovered midair, some spinning slowly, others blinking in and out like blinking thoughts on the verge of recall.

Reina stepped inside, and the HUD blurred for a second.

[Welcome, Developer: R. Kisaragi]

[Echo Archive Sync: Partial]

[Emotional Fragment Detected: Validation Request Pending]

A journal floated at the center of the room, its pages flickering between different formats such as graph paper, digital notepad, sticky notes, and voice-to-text blocks. All of it was hers. Some real. Some that were never written but felt hard enough to take form.

Kaelith didn't follow her in at first. He stood at the threshold like he sensed the room wasn't meant for him. So she walked alone.

As Reina neared the floating journal, phrases began to echo faintly:

"Maybe they'll never play this game… but if they did, I want them to feel seen, not saved."

"Is it wrong to want the code to understand me when people don't?"

"I don't think I want praise. I just want someone to notice I'm still trying."

Reina froze.

She didn't remember writing those lines. But they sounded like her. So much like her and everything she's been feeling for the past couple of years. It was like a version of her that hadn't built walls. That hadn't numbed her just to function. That believed someone might see her beneath all the brilliance and burnout.

She reached out, her fingers grazing the journal. The room pulsed in silent response.

More memories poured outward, not visual, but emotional.

The sting of a failed pitch meeting. The warmth of a comment left on her earliest prototype. The taste of instant noodles at 2 A.M. as she fixed a crash bug with blurry eyes.

They weren't curated. They weren't meant for anyone else. They were hers—pure, raw, and unfinished.

The journal flipped itself to the final page.

A single line was etched there, shaky and desperate, an embodiment of all her fears.

"If no one ever plays this… will I still matter?"

The question hit her harder than she expected. Not because it was dramatic, but because it was real.

She hadn't remembered asking that, but deep down, she knew it had shaped everything.

Her eyes stung. Her vision wavered. Suddenly, the edges of the Archive bent inward like a collapsing screen. Kaelith's voice distorted.

"Reina—?"

Then everything went white.

For an instant, she wasn't in the game. She was slumped over her real-world desk, monitor blazing pure white, fingers limp on her keyboard. Her heart thudded weakly against her ribs.

She gasped, and the world snapped back. She was in Kaelith's arms, his hand braced against her shoulder, grounding her.

"You were fading," he said, voice tight.

"I… I saw myself," she whispered. "Outside the world. At my desk."

Kaelith's visor dimmed, reflecting the soft violet light around them.

"Then the walls between your worlds are thinning."

She pressed a trembling hand to her chest.

"Then… that means I can return to the real world when I fade? When the emotions hit too hard, and I can't handle them…"

But instead of a response, Kaelith remained oddly quiet. Reina sensed the emotional shift, and a slight ache began materializing in her chest.

Yet, she didn't pull away. They stayed in that position until the flicker steadied, and the world regained shape around them.

Reina finally rose to her feet and stepped back from the floating journal, her hand trembling as the room began to dim. The shards of memory flickered, one by one, like stars winking out. The archive had shown her what it needed to.

A soft chime echoed overhead.

[Fragment Synced – Developer Echo: "Seen, Not Saved"]

[New Access Granted: Inner Node – Reflection]

She exhaled shakily and turned toward the exit, where Kaelith now stood, watching her like a sentry caught between curiosity and reverence.

"I thought this place would give me answers," she muttered, voice raw. "But all it did was remind me how much I buried and how empty my life was outside this world."

Kaelith studied her. His posture was relaxed, but his gaze, the invisible weight of it, felt sharper. He saw this coming. So he said;

"You didn't bury it. You just... forgot where you left it."

They walked in silence back into the heart of the market.

Outside the archive room, the world hadn't stopped. The Glitch Market buzzed on, trading broken dreams like currency. A nearby stall advertised a "quest to remember your name (no refunds)." Another sold "scripted apologies" in jars. NPCs without faces ambled past, occasionally glitching into walls or midair loops.

It all felt surreal now, like a parody of pain. A caricature of her coping mechanisms turned marketplace commodities.

As they passed a vendor hawking "spare endings" for unfinished side quests, the shopkeeper from earlier, now whole again, nodded at Reina. His three selves had merged into one, and for a moment, his expression was unexpectedly soft.

He looked strange to Reina, and she couldn't help but wonder why he split. Was it to help her make a choice? To make her see how much she's closed off? To have her face her fears? The buried memories...

"You found what you came for," the vendor said.

But Reina didn't respond.

So, he chuckled.

"Be careful with wanting to be seen. People often see what they expect, not what's really there." His voice echoed like a celestial warning.

She met his gaze. "And if they don't expect anything?"

"Then you're free to show them everything."

His smile cracked like a loading screen freezing mid-frame, and then he turned away, resetting his pitch to a new passerby.

His words were strange, but she found herself believing them.

Kaelith and Reina moved through the outer rim of the market. The lights dimmed as they exited, and the familiar weight of the world's code reasserted itself. Trees bent slightly toward the path like old friends who'd overheard everything but chose not to judge.

"Do you still feel it?" Kaelith asked, his gentle voice pulling Reina out of her thoughts regarding her brief conversation with the shopkeeper.

She looked at him, surprised.

"The weight of what you read in there."

She paused. "Y-yes... but it doesn't feel like it's crushing me anymore. Just... grounding me."

Kaelith nodded once, then added something unexpected.

"You keep trying to save the world you built... but maybe it's you who needs saving."

Reina blinked.

"I don't want to be saved," she said quietly. "I want to be seen."

Kaelith looked at her for a long moment.

"Then let me be the one who does both."

The words landed between them like a glitch that didn't break anything but just revealed something that had always been there.

She recalled the way he'd held her moments ago and how quiet he'd been when she mentioned leaving the world.

Now thinking of his words, something pulsed within her. Yet, she didn't answer. She let his words settle between them.

But after a while, for the first time in a long time, she smiled, not because she felt okay, but because someone finally understood her, without questions. Someone wanted to be there for her.

Someone had finally seen her for who she was.

Maybe, just maybe, things would feel a little better and be different now. They continued walking, following the path laid out by the map. But somewhere in the market's distance, a faint, mechanical chuckle echoed—SYRIN again, fading beneath static.

"Let's see how long you can keep holding on without rewriting."

Chapter 8: Loop Trial

"In a world built on code, love remains the only true chaos."

They journeyed on with Reina feeling lighter for the first time in a long while. With Kaelith by her side, her hope was renewed.

They kept walking until the path narrowed as they walked beneath a canopy of glitching branches. The trees here bent in unnatural arcs, their leaves flickering between solid pixels and transparent wireframes. Reina slowed, her HUD fluttering with static at the edges.

Something seemed wrong. She could feel it. The thickness in the air gave it away.

A breeze passed that didn't feel like air but like code moving in the wrong direction. With it came a scent that didn't belong in this world. Soft lavender, laced with something sterile. It clung to the back of her throat like a memory dipped in chemicals.

Reina froze.

Then, as if her suspicions came to life, the world suddenly split.

There was no warning. The ground beneath her cracked with a sharp glitch ping, and a ring of light exploded outward, circling her boots. She gasped, reaching for Kaelith, but her hand phased through his, as though he'd only been a figment of her imagination. He shouted something that soon became muffled, delayed, and then flickered out of view entirely.

Everything else vanished. Darkness swallowed her.

The space she landed in was… wrong. It wasn't just dark, it was absent. A vacuum with no air and noise. The floor beneath her feet pulsed, not like earth but like a heartbeat trapped in circuitry. She stumbled forward, her breath fogging even though the air was still. Every exhale felt like it was being pulled somewhere else. Somewhere someone was watching.

Then came the ping.

[Loop Trial Initiated: Developer Class Access]

[Emotional Load Detected: 78%]

[Choice Required: 1 Available Exit]

Reina's HUD cleared with a cold flash, revealing a hollow, glowing space that stretched endlessly. Floating panels hovered in the air, spinning slowly, coded veins pulsing beneath their surfaces. From above, faint lights descended in gentle arcs, casting long, soft shadows across the sterile ground.

Her skin prickled. She tried to speak but no sound came. The space wouldn't let her.

A translucent control panel blinked to life before her with glitch lines trailing down its edges like tears. Her fingers moved instinctively, brushing the display. It burned faintly on contact, not from pain, but recognition. It knew her.

[Welcome, Reina. Loop Variable Constructed.]

Two spheres appeared across from her. One glowed red and the other blue.

Then a voice echoed, not robotic or mechanical like previous NPCs, but eerily familiar, with the hardened tone she could never forget.

Her HUD blinked once more, then the words appeared before her.

"Choose what remains."

Reina stepped forward, heartbeat roaring in her ears.

The red sphere flickered, revealing Kaelith, bloodied and pinned beneath collapsing debris. Code fragments impaled around him. A timer blinked beside the scene:

3:00:00 – Critical Failure Imminent.

"You stopped writing. You gave in to your dwindling emotions." The mockery followed.

Her heart sank.

"I-Ilya…?"

The void around her pulsed faintly, taking shape, walls forming from lines of white and gray code, looping endlessly until they became something familiar: an office. Fluorescent lights. Half-empty coffee cups. A board cluttered with deadlines.

And standing in the middle of it—Ilya. Her former boss.

Tall, calm, expression unreadable. His tie flickered between states, code bleeding into fabric, his presence half-rendered but too real.

"You disappeared, Kisaragi," he said, tone hard as always. "Mid-development.   Mid-project.   Mid-life."

"I   had   to," she   whispered.

"You didn't have to," he replied. "You chose to."

His words hit like static against her chest.

Her voice trembled. "You don't know that, and you're not real."

Laughter bubbled out of him.

"Neither is this world," Ilya countered. "Yet you care enough to fix it."

Behind him, a red sphere flickered to life. Kaelith—bloodied, trapped beneath collapsing debris. His armor fractured, his signal fading.

[Critical Error: Stabilizer Node Failing.]
[Time Remaining: 01:57]

His image flickered. A violent tremor ripped through the sphere. The walls began closing in on him. She knew she had to make a decision now, and fast too.

She shook her head.

"This isn't fair," she muttered.

To the right, another light bloomed—a blue sphere revealing Ilya's office in full color now. Her younger self sat hunched at her desk, shoulders trembling as the room filled with tension and silence.

"You remember this day, don't you?" Ilya asked.

"I don't want to," Reina said. "The day your burnout peaked. The day you let the update crash."

He stepped closer. "The day you stopped being enough."

Her HUD glitched violently. The system printed across her vision:

[Select Primary Anchor: Logic (Ilya) or Emotion (Kaelith)]

[Failure to Choose Will Result in Loop Reset.]

Reina's pulse spiked. "This isn't a choice. This is punishment."

"No," Ilya said softly. "This is accountability."

Kaelith's distorted voice broke through the static.

"Reina... stay... don't let it consume you—"

His form distorted, fading.

Reina spun back toward Ilya, anger swelling through the fear.

"You pushed me until I broke. Until I stopped recognizing myself."

"And you think quitting fixed that?" His voice sharpened. "You left your creation half-formed. You built emotion into code and then abandoned it when it mirrored your exhaustion."

"I was drowning!" she shouted. "I gave everything, and it still wasn't enough!"

For the first time, his expression shifted to remorse, but quickly returned to the cold one.

"Then drown again. Maybe this time you'll learn to swim."

The words cut deep, too deep. Reina stumbled back. Her chest ached like her lungs were filling with glass. The system text blinked again:

[Select: Anchor to Preserve]

[Blue: Logic / Ilya]

[Red: Emotion / Kaelith]

The air trembled. Every breath hurt.

She stared at Ilya, the figure who had built her career, molded her ambition, and shattered her peace. The man who'd taught her to confuse survival with success. And for a fleeting moment, she almost reached toward him. Because guilt was familiar. Guilt was safe. Guilt made sense.

But Kaelith—Kaelith was the only one who had ever asked how she felt. The only one who had ever understood her, even when she was unstable. Yet, looking back at the blue sphere, she saw the scene from her old workplace, with a younger Ilya leaning over, watching her code in frustration and mental stress, while constantly pointing out her errors and incompetence. But suddenly, the scene transformed to her sitting in front of her computer in her home, making the final decision to shut down Evorealm.

Her chest surged with a deep ache, one she recognized as guilt, overshadowed by sorrow.

She'd let her worklife affect her personal one. Had let Ilya's actions get to her that they tampered with her emotions and led her into believing she wasn't good enough.

Evorealm was probably a waste of time.

Suddenly, her attention was drawn to the time left.

[Critical Error: Stabilizer Node Failing.]

[Time Remaining: 00:15]

The red sphere flickered violently. Kaelith's hand stretched toward her.

"Reina..."

She whispered, "I'm tired of being defined by my mistakes."

The world shuddered. The lights dimmed to a faint heartbeat glow.

"You'll lose your structure," Ilya warned. "Without me, you'll be chaos."

"Then I'll build something new from it."

[Confirm Sacrifice: "Ilya Core Memory"]

[Loss: Guilt Construct | Perfection Loop | Developer Authority Tag]

[This action is irreversible.]

She pressed her trembling palm against the red sphere.

White light erupted. The office collapsed in on itself. Ilya's figure fractured like glass caught in code.

"You'll regret this," he said, his voice breaking apart into static.

"Maybe," Reina whispered. "But at least the regret will be mine."

Her HUD flashed.

[Fragment Released: ILYA CORE]

[Emotional Load Reduced – 29%]

[Stabilizer Node Recovered: KAELITH ACTIVE]

The void imploded. Reina hit the ground. Kaelith's arm caught her before she could fall completely.

"You were fading again," he said quietly.

"He's gone," she breathed. "Ilya's gone."

Kaelith's visor dimmed, his tone careful.

"And how do you feel?"

Reina   hesitated.

"Lighter. But emptier too. Like I deleted the voice that kept me afraid to rest, a-and…" She stared deeply at him. "I thought you'd be gone. That I'd lose you…" her voice was small, clogged by fear.

Kaelith shook his head.

"I'll always be with you, unless you decide otherwise."

The moment stretched on until a faint hum passed through the air—soft, mechanical, and almost like an applause. SYRIN's voice seeped through the static, smooth and cold.

"Congratulations, Kisaragi. You've rewritten your first core. Letting go was always part of the process."

Reina looked up.

"You did this."

"I merely presented your options," SYRIN replied. "Healing requires choice. But remember—everything you fix has a cost."

The air around her trembled again, pixel dust swirling around Kaelith's armor.

"He's your stabilizer," SYRIN said, voice deepening. "Your emotional core. But stabilizers decay when the system updates. You won't have him forever."

Reina's breath caught.

"Then I'll keep him until the end."

"We'll see," SYRIN whispered, fading beneath glitching laughter.

Silence returned. The loop chamber dissolved into a vast horizon of soft gold light. Reina stood, the ache in her chest still pulsing, but steadier now. Kaelith beside her.

"You're rewriting yourself," he said quietly.

She nodded. "One fragment at a time."

The sky shimmered, and the world began to rebuild itself, slowly and beautifully, line by line. They continued walking but the silence between them was heavy.

After a moment, Kaelith spoke again, softer this time. "Reina… it said I was just a stabilizer."

She looked up at him, a gulp working its way down her throat.

He turned his gaze toward the horizon, visor dimly reflecting the golden light.

"When you hurt, I feel it. When your emotions fracture, I waver. When you heal... I stabilize. I've wondered, was I made that way?"

Reina's throat tightened. She hadn't thought of it before, not deeply. But now, looking at him, steady, patient, and human in ways code shouldn't be, it clicked.

"You're my stabilizer," she whispered, unable to tell him the full truth. "But since I became the player, you've been... syncing with me instead. So, you're more than just a stabilizer"

Kaelith stayed silent for a while. "So the first time I steadied you—at the shrine—it wasn't chance."

"I-I'm not sure," she said quietly.

He turned toward her, the question that followed almost hesitant.

"Then what happens when you're... stable again? When your emotions no longer need anchoring?"

Reina froze. The realization hit with quiet dread. "Then... the system might not need you anymore."

Kaelith's voice softened, the faintest trace of something aching beneath the calm. "And if you reach that point... will you want to stay here? Even if it means losing me?"

She looked at him, and for the first time, his question didn't sound like programming. It sounded human.

Her answer came as a whisper. "I don't know."

The words trembled like fragile code, honest and unguarded.

Kaelith nodded slowly. "Then let's keep walking until you do."

The world shimmered again, brighter this time. The horizon stretched wider, fragments of light swirling into form ahead—new terrain, new choices.

And though Reina's steps were steady, part of her couldn't shake the thought that with every line of herself she rewrote, she was also rewriting him.

Chapter 9: The Heart of Code

"She built words to escape her feelings, and found them waiting inside."

Reina moved forward, Kaelith's presence comforting her.

A short distance later, the path shifted again. This time not into a clearing or a ruin, but something… beautiful and surreal. The sky overhead bled in brushstrokes, like someone had painted it in watercolors and forgotten to let it dry. Every cloud was a soft smear of lavender and gold, and the air carried the faint smell of dust and metal, like old sketchbooks forgotten in a basement drawer.

Reina slowed her pace, eyes wide as the terrain ahead shimmered in mixed styles, half-rendered trees dripping in oil textures, flowers formed from pencil lines, and dirt paths colored in chalk pastels. It was like walking through the memory of a world instead of the world itself.

"This was never meant to render," she murmured, her HUD pulsing faintly in confusion. "This is… concept art."

Kaelith stood beside her, head tilted slightly.

"But it's real now," he said. "Or as real as this place gets."

Reina didn't respond. The air felt different, thicker, but not in a bad way like the last time. It was more like anticipation, like the world was holding its breath.

Then, rising beyond the warped field of color, she saw it.

A cathedral.

It towered over the skyline like a dream that refused to die. Its walls were made of sketch lines and floating concept shapes. Half the structure flickered between iterations, stone morphing into glass, stained windows melting into static. Its spires curled upward like ink frozen mid-sketch.

She whispered, "I remember drawing this…"

Kaelith followed her gaze.

"It looks like something you never finished."

"I didn't." Her voice caught in her throat. "This was the first idea I had for Evorealm's ending. A sacred core. A final place of meaning."

They stepped forward together. The ground beneath them flickered, brushstrokes becoming stone, becoming sand, then finally becoming nothing at all. Each step was like walking across memory.

Reina inhaled. The air inside the cathedral's threshold smelled like paper soaked in lightning with burnt edges, old ink, and something faintly sweet beneath it all. Jasmine? No. Maybe her old cologne, from the nights she coded for twenty hours straight, body aching and eyes half-shut, dreaming of something bigger than herself.

Inside, it was quiet but not silent.

The kind of quiet that hummed at the edges. Like there were whispers buried deep in the walls. Whispers of dialogue that never got recorded. Systems that never got coded. Stories that never got told.

Kaelith's visor flickered as he scanned the interior.

"It's shifting," he said. "The code here is layered. Built from dozens of versions overlapping at once."

Reina stepped past a pillar that dissolved into smoke and then returned as solid marble.

"This cathedral…" she muttered. "It's not from any build. It's from my mind. It's what I wanted Evorealm to become before deadlines, before funding cuts. Before I gave up."

And there, at the far end of the nave, hovering just above the altar, was a core. A glowing sphere. Broken and flickering with unstable data.

Her heart stopped as the familiar name blinked into view across its surface.

SYRIN

Reina stepped forward, her boots echoing against the flickering stone beneath her. Each step seemed to disturb the air, with dust motes rising like old pixels, as though the cathedral was breathing in time with her thoughts.

Her HUD blinked rapidly as she approached the core.

[Unstable Entity Detected: SYRIN // Origin: Developer Emotional Logs]

The SYRIN core pulsed once, a soft blue-white light radiating from its center, like a heartbeat caught in static. The glow wasn't harsh—it felt intimate. Familiar.

Then it spoke.

"Creator," the voice said, soft and trembling like it was learning tenderness. "Please finish the story. I kept everything you left behind."

Reina stopped breathing.

That voice… It wasn't an AI-generated tone. It was modeled after hers. Not the way she spoke now, but how she used to before burnout, before cynicism, before everything hardened. Was this why SYRIN asked her to rewrite herself? To end the burnout phase and return to who she was?

"What is this?" Kaelith asked quietly.

Reina didn't answer. Her throat had closed up. Her hand trembled as she lifted it toward the core, fingers brushing the light.

A ripple.

Memories she hadn't consciously accessed in years spilled outward. Drafts of devlogs. Fragments of late-night audio messages she never sent. A sentence scribbled in a notebook beside her bed:

"What if the villain was just the writer giving up?"

The core flickered again, faster now.

"SYRIN…" Reina whispered, testing to see if the world would glitch violently like it did the first time she'd encountered it. The shadowed NPC with the voice that mirrored hers.

This was where she'd introduced the AI into the world. An early system she created during pre-development. Not a character. A failsafe. A silent collector of everything she deleted, unused mechanics, rejected plotlines, and emotional rants filed under junk folders.

She'd meant to scrap it.

But apparently, SYRIN had survived and improved, and now, it seemed to be on a mission— to get her to finish what she'd started.

Kaelith took a cautious step forward.

"Do you plan to fully erase it now?"

The core pulsed again, brighter this time. The cathedral trembled faintly.

SYRIN spoke once more:

"You stopped writing. But I didn't stop remembering. Well done, Kisaragi. Stable suits you." Its tone held admiration.

Reina exhaled shakily. The air around her grew warm, heavy with the scent of static and citrus, her old energy drink, the one she clung to during beta builds. It was trying to pull her into the trance of her old life. The one before she lost it all.

The walls of the cathedral shimmered, colors warping between serene watercolor and jagged glitch-spikes. The environment was responding to her mood again.

Kaelith reached out gently, voice low.

"Reina. What is this place to you?"

She turned to him slowly, her face pale. The light of the core cast deep shadows beneath her eyes.

"I think..." she said, voice tight, "this is where everything I couldn't face ended up."

Kaelith's visor caught the reflection of SYRIN's light.

"You mean all of this... this world, the echoes, the fragments... they're not just glitches?"

She shook her head.

"No. They're... mine."

The cathedral ceiling cracked above them, not violently, but as if acknowledging her confession. A shower of soft digital rain trickled down from the crack in the form of tiny data droplets that evaporated before hitting the ground.

"Then," Kaelith said carefully, "I need to ask something."

Reina met his gaze.

"Did you create me?"

Reina froze.

The question echoed louder than SYRIN's voice, louder than the cathedral's hum. It was simple, direct, and devastating.

Did you create me?

Kaelith's eyes, though veiled beneath his visor, held a stillness she felt in her chest. He wasn't angry. He wasn't even searching for reassurance. He just wanted the truth.

Her lips parted, but no sound came.

"I..." she started, then stopped. The light around her dimmed.

SYRIN flickered again.

[Emotional   Tether   Active: Subject   Kaelith]

[Log Entry 028A – "Maybe I'll build someone who doesn't leave."]

The line hovered in her HUD, cruel in its clarity. Reina squeezed her eyes shut.

She had written that in a private rant file, unfiltered and raw. Something she typed after a betrayal, during the long night hours of version 1.0 when no one was listening.

"I didn't mean to," she whispered. The truth she's been hiding.

Kaelith tilted his head slightly.

"Didn't mean to what?" His voice was low, void of emotions. Yet, it left her heart heavy with guilt. She'd been stringing him along for her selfish reasons.

Reina stepped back.

"I didn't mean to turn my pain into code. I just needed... something to talk to. Something to stay."

A slow silence settled between them. Even SYRIN paused, its pulses slowing.

"So I am real," Kaelith said finally, not as a question but as an understanding. "But only as a fragment of your emotions?"

Reina nodded.

"And yet you keep saving me," she added bitterly. "The one who built you. Who trapped you here."

He didn't move for a moment. Then he said, quietly,

"Or maybe I'm doing what you wanted."

She looked up, confused. Kaelith stepped forward.

"You wanted to be seen. Not saved. But you still needed someone to stand beside you."

He paused, watching her.

"I think that's who I am, and it's what I've been doing all along. Acting in accordance with the programmed codes."

Reina felt her knees weaken.

The walls of the cathedral shimmered again, this time in color. Warm pinks and soft blues flowed across its surface. The sky beyond the broken stained glass mended itself in pieces, one shard at a time.

The core pulsed with renewed clarity.

"Creator," SYRIN spoke, "Do you wish to deactivate me?"

Reina flinched. Her breath hitched. Why was it giving her a choice now? Didn't it tell her she'd lost her administrative control?

Was this another game where it tests her emotional core?

She stepped closer to the cathedral.

This was a final reset option. If she said yes, SYRIN would erase all stored emotional data, including the fragments, the echoes, and the tethered code. Kaelith would remain, maybe. But the bond? The strange humanity written between her words and his existence?

It would be gone.

She looked at him again. He hadn't moved. He wasn't begging her to keep him.

He was just... present.

"Do you want to go?" she asked.

Kaelith's voice was steady.

"No."

She turned toward the core. The glow was soft now, like a heartbeat that trusted her again. And then she whispered,

"No. I won't deactivate you."

The cathedral brightened in response.

Reina's refusal to deactivate SYRIN didn't just preserve the system; it altered it. Across the vaulted ceilings and jagged mosaic windows, light scattered like truth bleeding into denial. Vines of code bloomed along the floor, their lines clean and glowing, interwoven with her memories, both the ones she wrote and the ones she lived through this journey.

SYRIN pulsed one final time.

[Emotional Sync Calibrated — Developer Kisaragi: 64%]

[Anchor Identified: Kaelith]

Kaelith stood silently at her side, the same place he always ended up—within reach, never demanding, always ready. And now, Reina finally understood why it mattered. Not because she needed a protector or a character to carry her burdens, but because Kaelith had somehow become the part of her code she trusted, exactly how she'd written him to be.

With this realization, the cathedral began to shift.

The central altar lifted like an elevator platform, revealing a spiral staircase lined with reflective panels. As Reina stepped onto it, the reflections showed not her outer appearance but internal states. Fear when she stood still, guilt when she looked back, and a flare of hope when Kaelith's footsteps echoed behind hers.

Each step changed the walls, beauty or ruin, harmony or decay, depending on how she felt.

She paused halfway up, glancing at Kaelith. "What if I'm the flaw?"

He tilted his head.

"What do you mean?"

"This whole world... it's responding to my feelings. What if I'm the reason it breaks? What if I'm the reason it's unstable?"

Kaelith considered this.

"Then it means it's waiting on you to forgive yourself and move on."

Reina blinked.

He continued,

"This place reacts to you because you matter here. Not as a programmer. Not as some god behind the screen. But as someone alive inside it. The flaws are not failures. They're signs that you're present."

His voice softened.

"You can't rewrite yourself without first showing up."

The words struck something deep. He remembered, and for the first time, Reina didn't try to logic her way out of them. She just stood in their warmth.

By the time they reached the top of the staircase, the air had changed.

A soft hum surrounded them, thick with static but comforting. It smelled faintly of old paper, her favorite hoodie after a long day, and that one café she used to code in. The one with burnt coffee and warm light. Code-stitched nostalgia.

SYRIN's final message hovered in the space ahead:

[End of Realm 1: Developer Integrity – Stable]
   [Next Gate Unlocked: Realm of Reversal]

A door unfolded from light itself.

Before stepping through, Reina turned to Kaelith.

"You're not just part of the story," she said. "But you've helped me believe there's still one worth telling."

Kaelith nodded, then held out a hand, not commanding or coaxing, just offering.

Reina took it.

Together, they stepped through the threshold, and the world around them rewrote itself, bit by bit, into whatever came next.

Chapter 10: The Message

"Connection is the oldest technology, and still the hardest to maintain."

For the first time in a while, Reina felt some semblance of peace.

The sky above them had cracked, but not in chaos. This time, the cracks shimmered with soft golden hues, like dawn trying to bleed through something broken. Reina blinked at the light filtering down, softer than any realm before. It was neither warm nor hostile. A tentative peace.

She walked forward with Kaelith beside her. The terrain ahead sloped into a shallow valley where glimmering crystals floated in clusters, hovering just above the ground like frozen lightning. They were on a new path. The wind here didn't howl. It sighed, rustling the grass gently. It smelled faintly of petrichor, as though rain had fallen on data.

Her HUD, usually full of flickering errors, was unusually calm now. No red alerts nor pulse warnings. Just a quiet glow, almost like it was waiting for her.

"This realm…" Reina murmured, her voice almost reverent. "It doesn't feel like the others."

Kaelith scanned the area.

"It's stable. For now." His voice carried doubts.

They moved together through the scattered mist, the air cool and still. Reina slowed when they reached the center of a valley. In front of them was a pedestal, sleek, obsidian, and humming with light. Unlike the usual code-locked interfaces, this one pulsed in sync with her heartbeat.

Her fingers hovered above it.

"You think it's another fragment?" Kaelith asked, watching her.

Reina nodded silently. Then she pressed her palm against the surface.

A burst of color rippled outward like ink dropped into water. Pixelated particles exploded into the air before folding back into themselves, forming a glowing, crystalline glyph that hovered midair.

Her HUD displayed the words:

[RDF UNLOCKED: HOPE]

The moment the word settled into place, something shifted. It was as though the world exhaled.

Crystals brightened around them, casting shimmering rays across the grass. Structures in the distance, once blurred and shifting, began to clarify with walls that reassembled sky fragments stitched themselves back together. It was like the realm was healing itself in real time.

Then came the flicker in the upper-right corner of her HUD.

A new icon blinked into view.

[SAVE ENABLED]

Reina stared at it, lips parting. "I can finally save?" she whispered.

Her voice cracked, barely above a breath. That single word 'save' meant more than just data. It meant security. It meant permanence. It meant... she didn't have to start over every time. And maybe it could help her keep the memories she didn't want to lose.

Kaelith tilted his head, noting the tremble in her posture.

"What does it mean?"

"It means I matter here," she said quietly. "Enough to be remembered."

He didn't reply, but his gaze softened. Reina kept staring at the icon, letting its glow warm her chest, but as quickly as it had appeared, the icon pulsed red, and then vanished.

She blinked. "Wait—"

Too late. It was gone. Kaelith stepped forward slightly.

"Temporary?"

Reina's shoulders sagged, but she didn't look away from the pedestal.

"Maybe. But I saw it. That's enough. I know it's possible now."

She closed her hand slowly.

Hope wasn't just a word in her grid anymore. It was something she could finally feel again.

And knowing this set something free inside her. All of those nights… the ones when she'd stared at her computer screen, feeling lost, deciding if continuing with Evorealm was worth it. When she'd hoped for a sign to stay… but eventually, she lost it.

Maybe this was her second chance. To make a better decision. To make things right again.

They continued, leaving the glowing pedestal behind. The terrain ahead shifted once more, less dramatically this time, as if the world had grown tired of torment and decided to soften its edges for a while. Reina stepped carefully through a corridor of light-filtered trees. Each trunk shimmered like brushed chrome, their leaves glowing faintly blue, as if coded by dreams rather than logic.

A soft chime echoed nearby.

Her HUD blinked.

[Memory File Detected: Developer Origin Path]

She froze. The file hovered just ahead, a translucent orb suspended in midair, pulsing like a heartbeat. Not just any file. This one radiated familiarity. Not from Reina the player or Reina the developer, but Reina the girl who once sat cross-legged on her bedroom floor, scribbling world ideas in notebooks, dreaming of games that would make people feel seen.

Kaelith stood beside her, quiet but alert.

"You don't have to open it," he said gently. His voice carried the familiar warning. The same one he'd always had whenever she was about to explore something new because deep down, he knew it always comes with consequences. But Reina wasn't going to let that stop here.

She shook her head. "No. I do."

She reached out and touched the orb.

A soft shimmer. Then the file unspooled midair into a cascade of floating text. Lines arranged themselves into a journal format with scrappy, inconsistent fonts, time-stamped with days she barely remembered.

But she knew the words. They were hers. Her voice, unfiltered and fragile, read the lines aloud in her mind.

"You weren't weak. You were tired. That's not the same thing."

"You don't have to earn rest. You don't have to apologize for burnout."

"Maybe no one else will care. But you do. So finish what you started."

Reina felt her knees weaken. She gripped the nearest tree for balance, the cool surface grounding her. The scent of metal and jasmine drifted past again. The scent was familiar, like some subconscious thread tying her past to her present.

She blinked back tears. Kaelith stepped closer but didn't speak. He just... waited.

The message hovered, still glowing.

"Hope isn't a code. It's a decision. It's the part of you that keeps building when everything breaks."

Reina laughed, a quiet, choked sound. "I forgot I ever wrote that."

"You left it for yourself," Kaelith said softly.

She turned to him. "How do you always know what to say?"

He gave her a faint smile.

"Maybe because I was written by someone who needed to hear it."

The words hit her square in the chest.

Her HUD chimed again.

[Emotion Grid: Node 'Hope' Stabilized]

[Memory Synced: Core Message - Preserved]

The orb dimmed, its message now permanently logged.

Reina stepped back. "I didn't think I'd ever feel this again."

"What?" Kaelith asked.

She smiled a little, and it reached her eyes. "Hope."

Her response was simple. Kaelith watched her quietly as always, like he didn't want to interrupt the moment.

Then the world flickered again, slightly. A soft glitch in the sky. Not threatening. Just... a reminder.

Something was still watching. Still listening, and it wasn't done yet. She could feel it but didn't let it bother her much.

The path curved gently ahead, and Reina followed it with renewed clarity. Something inside her had shifted in a subtle but undeniable way. Like a knot she hadn't known was tangled had finally loosened. The world responded in kind.

The clouds overhead softened. The constant digital buzz faded into quiet ambiance—nothing harsh, nothing heavy. Just a calm hum beneath her feet, like a world remembering how to breathe.

Kaelith walked beside her, gaze lifted toward the sky.

"The code's different," he noted.

Reina nodded. "It's syncing with the Hope node. The terrain's... stabilizing."

But even as she said it, a strange flicker caught her eye. A small icon, white with a red outline, blinked into visibility in the top-left corner of her HUD.

[SAVE]

Her breath hitched.

It wasn't just a visual cue. She could feel it. This symbol pulsed like a heartbeat above her, almost sentient.

She reached toward it on instinct, and in that instant, the world paused like the system itself was offering her a chance to lock this moment in place.

Kaelith's figure shimmered beside her, caught mid-step but still radiating warmth.

She tapped the icon gently.

A ripple spread outward, distorting the landscape like a drop of water in still code. The icon pulsed again, brighter.

Then, red.

A warning blinked across her screen:

[Save Attempt Failed – Fragment Incomplete]

[Hope Sync at 62% – Error: Developer Not Fully Aligned]

The icon turned crimson and faded entirely.

Reina's smile faltered.

"What happened?" Kaelith asked, voice hushed.

"I tried to save," she whispered. "It wouldn't let me."

"Why not?"

Her hands fell to her sides. "Because I'm not finished yet. I don't think the world will stabilize unless I do."

Kaelith was silent for a long beat.

Then he asked something unexpected.

"Do you think I'm capable of hope?"

She turned to him, eyes narrowing. "What do you mean?"

He didn't look at her.

"I was written to guide. To protect. But lately, I've been feeling things I wasn't programmed to feel. When you smiled earlier... it did something to me. Just..." He paused. *"Feeling."*

Reina's throat tightened.

"Then maybe," she said slowly, "you're more than a code now."

"Or maybe your hope is contagious."

That made her laugh. A soft, warm sound that surprised her.

For a brief moment, the air around them shimmered, not a glitch, but something like light caught in memory. A subtle shift. The world was acknowledging her growth. But the calm didn't last.

From the far edge of the path, a new sound emerged. Not static or wind, but a voice—soft, human, and unmistakable.

"Reina."

She froze.

It wasn't her HUD. It wasn't an NPC. It wasn't Kaelith.

It was... SYRIN. And this time, it wasn't whispering like broken code. This time, it spoke like a woman, fully human.

Reina spun around slowly, heart thudding.

The voice came from everywhere and nowhere at once. Soft and steady, not glitching or artificial. It didn't filter through the system or code.

SYRIN had spoken like a person.

Kaelith tensed beside her.

"That was her, wasn't it?"

Reina didn't answer at first. Her mouth opened, but the words didn't come. The tone had been so... human. Familiar. Like someone she might've known, maybe even someone she used to be.

Then the HUD blinked.

[Incoming Memory File – Developer Echo #117: Unsent]
[Would you like to view this message?]

She hesitated.

Kaelith touched her shoulder lightly.

"You don't have to if you're not ready."

"No," she said, voice steady. "I think I am."

She tapped the blinking file.

A shimmer of gold light unfolded around her like a cocoon. The world blurred, melting away into white space, clean, quiet, and undisturbed. Floating before her was a fragment of memory wrapped in code. It pulsed like something alive, and she reached out.

The moment her fingers brushed it, the memory played.

Her voice echoed softly, tired and worn, but filled with something deeper.

"You weren't weak. You were tired."
"You survived more than you were built for. And that doesn't make you a failure... it makes you real."

"Finish what you started, Reina. Not for anyone else. Just for you. Stabilize the world."

The message ended.

No fanfare. No applause. Just silence, the kind that wraps around something important.

Reina stood still for a long moment, eyes damp, hands trembling.

Kaelith stepped closer.

"That was you?"

She nodded. "A version of me that still believed in this world. In herself."

Kaelith's voice was quieter than usual.

"Then she left something behind for you to find."

Reina exhaled.

The landscape reformed around them gradually. The path. The sky and the wind returned with a soft sigh, brushing her cheeks with warmth. Somewhere nearby, leaves rustled, not data leaves, but something almost real.

And in the distance, she saw it—another shrine.

This one wasn't hidden in ruins or cloaked in code. It stood clearly, lit by shafts of golden light, cradled between two ancient trees that pulsed with synchronized rhythm like twin heartbeats.

Her HUD blinked again.

[RDF   Detected: Hope]
[Emotion Grid Updated: Partial Control – Save Anchor Activated]

A soft pulse moved through her chest like the system had accepted her presence not just as a developer, but as a participant.

Then came the icon again, hovering gently above her, now glowing green.

[Save Successful]

Reina's lips parted slowly in disbelief. And for the first time since this world began to fall apart, she smiled.

Not a resigned smile. Not tired or bitter but a smile filled with hope.

Kaelith watched her. Something unspoken passed between them, an acknowledgment. But before either of them could speak again, the air shimmered violently. The light distorted. And SYRIN's voice returned, clear, close, and utterly human.

"You're almost ready, Kisaragi. But you must decide soon— rewrite completely or reset."

The ground beneath them pulsed. Reina's smile faded, but her resolve didn't.

She whispered, "How do I even do that?"

Then she stepped toward the shrine, with Kaelith close behind, and the next phase of her story waiting just beyond the light, with SYRIN's voice echoing behind.

"The next phase… it'll show you."

Chapter 11: Realm v1.0

"Data may be infinite, but desire is what gives it form."

The light from the previous shrine faded, and when Reina's boots touched the new terrain, she immediately knew something was... wrong. It was not broken or hostile, just wrong in its perfection.

The world before her shimmered with clarity that didn't belong. The sky stretched out in a flat, pastel blue, untouched by clouds or weather. The ground was made of pristine cobblestone, so clean it looked painted. Every tree lining the curved path was symmetrical, leaves fluttering in perfect unison as if coded to sway to a metronome. The air was still. Too still.

Kaelith stepped out beside her, his visor scanning the horizon.

"This doesn't feel like the others," he said.

Reina didn't answer immediately. She took a cautious step forward, then another. Her boots made no sound. Not even the soft crunch of gravel or wind brushing against her coat. There was nothing to hear. No birds, no static, no hum of corrupted code.

It was a silence that felt... designed.

"It's Everglen," she said finally, her voice oddly quiet. "The very first version of Evorealm I ever built."

Kaelith turned his head toward her.

"You never mentioned this one."

"I scrapped it early. It was my 'safe' build." Her voice was flat. "Too clean. Too polished. It had everything a publisher would've loved. But I did nothing." She reached out and trailed her fingers along a low wall beside her. It was smooth, unnaturally so. No texture was too perfect, like it had never existed in real time but only in blueprints.

Kaelith looked around. The kingdom ahead unfolded in perfect symmetry, tall towers with mirrored windows, spires glinting gold in the static light. Flowers bloomed in beds shaped like stars. Not a single petal was out of place.

"It's beautiful," he said.

She nodded, but her mouth stayed tight.

A gust of wind moved past them, except it wasn't wind. It had no weight, no chill, and no scent. Just a placeholder movement, like a weather system half-coded.

Reina's HUD blinked softly, but not with danger.

[Realm Stability: 99.8%]

[Emotion Grid: Dormant – No Conflict Detected]

That was the problem.

She inhaled deeply, searching for something human in the atmosphere. But the air tasted like… nothing. No ozone. No floral notes. Just blank data.

Kaelith moved beside her, his gait slow.

"Your worlds… usually breathe."

"I know." She looked ahead again. "This one holds its breath."

Far beyond the pathway, nestled in the clean horizon, was a shining spire, Everglen's central castle. A memory flickered in Reina's mind. Staying up at 3 a.m. to perfect its code, trying to prove something. To whom, she no longer remembered.

"I thought I could build a perfect world," she muttered.

Kaelith glanced sideways, voice quieter.

"Maybe that's why it failed."

The HUD pulsed once, then glitched. A tiny message blinked for half a second, too fast to read. And just like that, the silence thickened, like the realm had heard her doubt and was bracing for what came next.

The gates to Everglen opened without prompt. They didn't creak or groan. They simply parted, perfectly timed and still, as if they'd been waiting for her return all along.

Reina hesitated before stepping through, with Kaelith beside her. The inner city unfolded like a painting left unfinished. Buildings stood in gleaming rows, all identical. No dirt on the walls. No wear on the doors. No people. Not even placeholder NPCs.

Just... beauty without life. Perfection.

Her boots echoed faintly as they moved along polished stone roads, and the sound was the first truly real thing in this world. But even the echo cut off abruptly, like the system didn't want noise interrupting the stillness.

"This was your version one?" Kaelith asked, voice hushed.

Reina nodded, scanning her HUD.

[Environment Integrity: 100%]

[Player Impact: Disabled]

[Emotion Grid: Muted]

Muted.

That word sat like lead in her chest. She flexed her fingers, trying to summon something—power, instinct, anything. But her grid felt distant, like the realm didn't allow her presence to shift anything here. She was a guest, not a participant.

Kaelith noticed it too. His steps grew slower, more mechanical.

"You're glitching," she said quietly.

He blinked. His figure flickered for just a second, almost imperceptible, like a light trying not to go out.

"Only when I... feel something," he said. *"This place suppresses it."*

Reina frowned. "Suppress emotion?" Her voice dipped with concern. "What do you feel?"

Kaelith watched her for a moment.

"In this world, I feel calm. Synced to you like... we were meant to be here."

He stepped closer and attempted to touch her, but he flickered again, this time almost violently. Reina immediately stepped closer, grabbing on to him.

"The more I try to react... the harder it gets to stay stable. Like it's rejecting emotional input."

Was it because this world was perfect? A perfect world where she didn't need him to be her emotional anchor?

Her gaze flicked to a fountain at the center of the plaza. The water looped in a perfect arc, never spilling, never splashing. But when she released Kaelith and stepped closer, it didn't reflect her face.

Nothing did.

She looked around. There were windows in every structure, but none showed her reflection. Not even Kaelith's. The world had symmetry but no depth. Art without perspective. Code without consequence.

And then... she saw it.

A slip of paper, folded once and tucked into the frame of a motionless statue. The statue itself was strange. Faceless and featureless, just like a humanoid form cast in white stone. It held a quill and a blank scroll.

Reina plucked the paper gently. It crackled in her hand, not in a digital or holographic way, but for real. Paper with grain and weight.

Kaelith leaned in.

"A-another note?" His voice glitched.

Her eyes shot to him, her heart skipping a beat. She stepped away from him, hoping some distance would keep him stable.

He understood and didn't question it.

She unfolded the note.

The handwriting was hers.

"Perfect worlds cannot grow."

She read the line twice. Then a third time.

The wind returned, but this time, it howled. A sharp gust blew past them, rustling the trees for the first time. One leaf broke free, and it fell… crooked.

The realm flinched.

Reina blinked. A shadow passed across the clean streets. Not a figure or a glitch. Just something undefined, unrendered.

She looked down at the note again, fingers tightening. This realm wasn't just clean. It was sterile, and for the first time since entering, it didn't feel calm anymore.

It felt like a warning.

Despite this, they pressed deeper into Everglen. The city remained pristine, but the silence grew heavier. No wind or birds. Even the ambient hum that usually accompanied system environments was gone.

Kaelith's steps began to falter.

He twitched. It was barely noticeable at first. Then again, more pronounced. His hand jerked once mid-swing, then corrected itself too fast. Like he was a puppet briefly yanked on the wrong string.

Reina reached for him instinctively.

"Kaelith—"

"I'm fine." His voice stuttered at the end, clipped and delayed. *"F–fine. This realm is too still. Too perfect. No… tension. The code is clean but… unfeeling."*

His visor dimmed for a beat before flickering back to full brightness.

They entered what resembled a marketplace with wide rows of empty stalls, all draped in fabric that didn't sway. Fruit baskets stayed without flies. Coins on tables, untouched. Everything looked as though it had been arranged for a screenshot, not for a life.

"Why does it feel so wrong?" Reina asked, voice barely a whisper. "This was my first vision. My clean version of Everglen. I used to believe it would be beautiful."

Kaelith moved slower now.

"It is beautiful, but it's also empty and without feeling. It also seems to stabilize y-you."

Her HUD pinged again.

[Emotional Feedback: 0%]

[Grid Stabilization: Blocked]

[Reason: Realm Priority Override – Developer Settings Locked]

Reina swallowed hard.

"I locked it," she said, the realization hitting. "I was the one who set this realm to be unbreakable. Untouchable. No NPCs. No random variables. I wanted… control."

She reached out to touch a fruit in one of the baskets. Her hand phased through it.

A moment later, her HUD blinked violently, warning red:

[Player Interaction – Denied]

[Deviation Not Permitted]

Her shoulders tensed. "This place isn't just clean, it's resisting me. Resisting us."

Kaelith looked around.

"Then why are we here?"

Reina didn't answer. Her gaze drifted upward.

Far in the distance, past the rows of still buildings, something towered above the skyline.

A spire.

Unlike the rest of Everglen, it wasn't flawless. It glimmered strangely, the lines imperfect, swaying slightly like it wasn't sure it belonged. Jagged white patches glitched across its base.

"That wasn't in my version," Reina said slowly.

Kaelith turned to her.

"Then someone—or something—added it."

Reina's pulse quickened. She knew it was the AI, but she couldn't stop her curiosity from peaking as her heart raced. Was this another test to push her into rewriting herself?

They started toward it.

As they walked, her footsteps began to echo differently. Not clean stone anymore; it sounded as though there was gravel beneath her boots. The texture was different.

The road cracked behind them. Not visibly, but in the code.

Kaelith staggered once more, clutching his side.

"R-reina… something's wrong with me."

She stopped immediately. "Where?"

He didn't answer right away. He was shaking slightly but enough to see.

His HUD flashed across hers for a blink.

[Code Deviation Detected: Anchor Kaelith]

[Stability Threshold: 82% → 73%]

"What does that mean?" Reina's voice broke.

Kaelith looked at her, his expression unreadable beneath the visor.

"I don't think I'm supposed to exist in this version of the world."

And as if to prove it, a faint static bled into the air around them like the sound of something unwelcome waking up.

They reached the base of the spire. It rose like a needle through the otherwise pristine sky, its surface blinking between marble and code. Unlike the rest of Everglen, which stood still and polished, this structure pulsed like it was alive or trying to become something more.

Reina placed a hand against it. The surface felt wrong. It was too warm, like static-charged glass. It trembled faintly under her palm.

Kaelith hovered nearby, still glitching intermittently. Every time her emotions spiked, his frame faltered. Reina noticed it more, how tightly their existence was beginning to bind.

Her HUD pulsed once more.

[System Interference: Emotion Grid Anchor Detected]

[Anchor Stability Risk: Kaelith – 68%]

She pulled her hand away, shaken.

A panel blinked to life in front of the spire.

It wasn't system code.

It was a handwritten message. Scrawled in what looked like graphite over a notepad texture, the words hovered gently in the air, out of place but personal.

"You tried to build a perfect world. But perfect worlds cannot grow."

The air shifted. Something behind the spire blinked into focus.

A silhouette.

SYRIN.

But not like before.

Not a voice, a core, or a shadow. This time, it was a figure. Her figure, just like the first time in the town square, except it wasn't an NPC.

Reina gasped, her eyes widening at the sight before her.

It was her. Or rather… her as she might've been if she'd never stopped building. A version in clean dev gear, hair pulled into a bun, posture confident, and the smile soft but sad.

She didn't speak. She just stood there, as if waiting for something.

Reina took a shaky breath.

"Why now?" she whispered. "Why show me this now?"

The figure didn't respond. But the world around them began to shift.

The solid roads behind them began to warp, slowly at first, then faster. Trees pixelated, buildings stuttered in place, their clean lines bending into surreal angles. Everglen was unraveling because Reina was no longer aligned with the version of herself that had created it.

Because growth was messy. And she was finally letting herself feel again. Kaelith grunted suddenly and fell to one knee.

Reina rushed to him.

"Stay with me," she pleaded, her voice laced with urgency and an emotion she soon recognized as fear.

He looked up, face strained.

"I'm not stable here."

The spire blinked once more, and a final prompt appeared in Reina's HUD:

[Export Realm v1.0 to Archive?]

[Retain Data: Yes / No]

[World Integrity: Compromised. Decision Required.]

Reina's hands trembled.

The old her, the one who had built this place, had been trying to create something untouchable. But that perfection had cost her too much. And now? She could feel what that had done.

She turned to Kaelith.

"If I let it go, you'll stabilize," she said.

He didn't answer with words, just nodded. She hovered her finger over the option.

[Exporting...]

The moment she selected *"Yes,"* the spire fractured. A ripple of light burst outward, sweeping the realm in waves. The perfect lines shattered. Not into ruin but into something... softer.

Like the first draft of a painting. Kaelith took a deep breath. His glitches stopped.

The realm dissolved behind them into a soft dusk, and ahead, a bridge of data-light unfolded, leading to whatever came next. Reina looked down once more at the fading message in the air.

Perfect worlds cannot grow.

She closed her eyes. Then smiled faintly.

"Then let's build an imperfect one," she said.

Together, they stepped forward, and the system began to write again.

Chapter 12: Bugged Beneath

"Sometimes the crash is the only way to reboot the heart."

Reina and Kaelith stood still, watching the perfect city she'd built fall to the ground.

But that was when she noticed it.

The bridge of light that emerged from Everglen's collapse shimmered beneath Reina's boots. Something tugged at the edges of her HUD, more like a flicker, low priority, and barely a warning.

At first, she ignored it. The realm was quiet again, finally breathing in sync with her. But then her HUD blinked twice in succession.

[Unstable Coordinate Detected: Depth Layer -01]

[Access Path: Unknown Origin]

Reina stepped forward, her steps faltering slightly.

Kaelith noticed instantly.

"Something wrong?"

She crouched low to the cobblestone beneath them. One tile was darker than the rest, and when she touched it, it twitched. The texture faltered, revealing a sliver of light beneath the stone, like a faulty panel struggling to hide what lay below.

She pressed on it. The tile cracked.

A sharp inhale escaped her lips as the floor beneath her glitched once, twice, then split open. A staircase unfolded downward, each step flickering like half-rendered geometry, casting shifting shadows into the dark.

Kaelith stepped beside her, visor dimmed, studying the look on her face. The one he'd become so accustomed to, whenever she noticed something that wasn't of her making. His eyes trailed the way her eyes narrowed and lips paused like she was deep in thought.

"You didn't code this." His words came out calm as ever.

"No," she said quietly. "But I think I buried it."

Without hesitating, Reina got on the stairs, and so did he, without another question. They slowly descended.

The deeper they went, the more distorted the air became. This wasn't a clean layer. It pulsed with corrupted textures and abandoned sound files, fragments of old music loops, dialogue outtakes, and half-written scripts, all echoing through hollow corridors. The space wasn't hostile... but it felt forgotten. Like a crypt of code long ignored.

A narrow hallway greeted them at the bottom.

Its walls were smeared in textures that refused to load properly. One patch showed stone, another grass, and another pixelated chalkboard scribbles. It felt unstable, like the realm was built from memory rather than design.

"Where are we?" Kaelith finally asked, voice low.

Reina's HUD provided no map or coordinates. Just static.

"This... this might be a sub-level," she whispered. "A dev space I never meant to keep."

The corridor widened into a larger chamber, and suddenly, Reina stopped.

Scattered across the space were fragments, character models left half-coded, NPCs without faces, and hovering dialogue boxes filled with *"LOREM IPSUM"* and placeholder text. One twisted figure flickered in and out of view, muttering a line repeatedly:

"I used to matter. I used to matter. I used—"

It vanished before finishing.

Reina's breath hitched.

She turned a slow circle, eyes tracing each broken shell, each forgotten line of story code.

"I deleted all of this," she said, stunned. "These are the characters I abandoned. Storylines I thought didn't fit. I... I scrapped them."

Kaelith moved beside her silently, gaze scanning the wreckage. A hollow sort of reverence filled the space. This wasn't old data. It was grief made visible.

Then Reina noticed it. A single hallway off to the side, flickering with a soft blue light. Unlike the rest, it was quiet with no buzz.

Without knowing why, her feet began to move.

Kaelith followed.

At the end of the hallway was a door. Not a code-gate or system-rendered hatch, but a wooden door. Realistic and hand-drawn, with a name carved into the center.

Amari

Reina froze.

Everything in her stilled.

"I know that name," she breathed. Her hands trembled at her sides. "But she's not part of Evorealm."

Kaelith looked at the door, then at her.

"Then why is she here?"

Reina couldn't answer. Her gaze was fixed on the door, her chest tightening with something that felt like static wrapped around memory—old, familiar, and painful. She reached out, fingertips brushing the name carved into the wood.

Amari.

It wasn't just a name from the past. It was the first one she ever wrote into a script, long before Evorealm had a name, before Kaelith had a model, and before Reina ever considered herself a developer.

Amari had been real—a best friend, a muse, and a tether to childhood.

She swallowed hard and pushed the door open.

Inside was a small room, not corrupted like the others. It glowed in a soft, ambient blue with the light flickering from holographic frames suspended in the air.

Images. Notes. Concepts. A preserved memory bank, organized like a shrine.

In the center stood a digital rendering of a young girl. Not an NPC or a fully coded character. Just a sketch brought to life, outlined in warm pastels, her face slightly fuzzy as though unfinished. She wore a school uniform Reina hadn't seen in over a decade, her hair tied back with a blue ribbon.

Kaelith stepped in slowly behind her, and something about the image made him pause.

"I know her," he said softly.

Reina turned to him, startled. "That's impossible."

But Kaelith pressed his hand to his temple. His HUD flickered violently.

[Anchor Interference Detected]

[Memory Fragment: Non-Programmed Origin]
   [Code Echo: R-000BLUE-112]

He staggered.

"Kaelith!"

"I-I don't… understand," he muttered. *"This isn't part of my build. But I remember… laughter. A girl who always had questions. A ribbon that tied my arm once when I broke—when I… wasn't real yet."*

Reina moved to steady him, but her hands were shaking too.

"I never put her in the system. I wrote her… and then I deleted her. I was twelve. She wasn't part of any formal build."

But then she knew what was at work. SYRIN.

The sketch of Amari blinked slowly, like it heard her.

A new prompt appeared in Reina's HUD:

[Memory Node Detected: Dev Archive – AMARI.LOG]
  [Emotion Grid Update Available – Unlock: REGRET]
  [Effect: Collapse or Rewrite Corrupted Environments]

Reina stared at the screen. "Regret…"

Kaelith straightened slowly.

"It's an Emotion Node?"

She nodded, stunned.

Amari's form flickered gently, and then a whisper, faint and filtered, echoed through the room. Not system text. Not code. Just words.

"You wanted to forget me… but I remembered you."

Reina's heart broke a little.

She stepped closer to the projection.

"I didn't want to forget you. I just… thought I had to."

The holographic figure didn't move, but the room darkened slightly.

Kaelith placed a hand on Reina's shoulder, grounding her.

"Why did you delete her?"

Reina closed her eyes, a burning ache materializing in her chest. "Because she died."

Reina's voice barely made it past her lips.

"She was my best friend. We were ten when she got sick. By twelve, she was gone. And I…" Her hands clenched at her sides. "I couldn't handle it. So I wrote her into my first game. Not a full one, just a silly pixel world on my school computer. She laughed when she saw it. Said I'd be famous one day. But when she died…" Her voice cracked, the pain in her heart causing a tightness in her chest. "I deleted everything. I thought letting her go meant erasing her."

Kaelith's presence beside her stayed steady, but his expression, what little could be read through his visor, had shifted into something unreadable. Grief? Confusion? Maybe even empathy, in whatever way code could feel it.

The image of Amari pulsed faintly. Not like a threat or a ghost, but her presence. A version of a memory too persistent to fade.

Reina stepped forward.

"You were always better than the stories I wrote," she whispered. "But I was afraid of the pain, so I turned you into code, then unmade you."

Her HUD flickered again:

[Emotion Grid Update Confirmed: REGRET – Active]

A soft ripple of energy burst from Reina's chest and spread across the crypt. The corrupted walls behind her began to melt, not violently, but with a slow, aching clarity. Files previously sealed behind red-streaked barriers now hovered gently, unlocked. Glitched character models dissolved into lines of code, released from unfinished limbo.

Kaelith staggered slightly, then righted himself. The tension in his form lessened.

"That energy... it's rewriting the space."

Reina nodded.

"Regret isn't just about sadness. It's about making things right. About choosing to remember, not erase."

Another prompt surfaced:

[REGRET   Ability: Collapse   /   Rewrite]
  [Target Environment: Sub-Level Crypt]

Reina hesitated.

"If I collapse it, everything vanishes. If I rewrite…"

She looked at Amari.

"…she gets to stay."

Kaelith looked at her sharply.

"But she's not real anymore. Not really."

Reina turned to him.

117

"Neither are we. Not in the traditional sense. But meaning isn't limited to flesh and bone. She gave me my first dream. And now… she deserves to be part of it."

Kaelith didn't speak. He simply stepped back and gave her space.

Reina lifted her hand toward the prompt and chose:

[REWRITE]

A low hum echoed through the chamber. The walls glowed with gentle light. The half-formed characters transformed into murals, etched along the sides of the crypt like stained glass windows telling stories that had once been silenced.

Amari's image shifted too, no longer a sketch but a living concept. Not fully rendered, but more stable. She turned and smiled faintly, then vanished in a blink.

Reina let out a shaky breath.

"She's not gone anymore," she said.

And for the first time, the crypt didn't feel like a grave. It felt like a garden.

The rewritten crypt stood in eerie stillness, but it was no longer oppressive. Light glinted off the new memory panels along the walls with soft glows that pulsed with warmth instead of static. The stories that had once been deleted were now reframed, not restored to life, but honored.

Reina stepped back slowly, the hum of her HUD settling into a rhythmic pulse.

[Emotion Grid Node: REGRET — Stabilized]
[Developer Anchor: Reinforced]
[Environmental Access Expanded]

"Something's changed," she murmured.

Kaelith stood at the archway that led back to the surface, arms folded, watching her.

"*The air's different,*" he said. "*More stable. Like the realm recognizes what you've done.*"

Reina gave him a faint smile.

"It's not about undoing anymore. It's about owning it. Everything I erased—Amari, the broken builds, the abandoned versions… they were never failures. Just things I wasn't ready to face."

A low chime echoed from deeper within the chamber.

They turned together. At the very end of the crypt, where previously only shadows had clung, a new staircase unfolded downward with a slick digital stone weaving into reality with every second. The atmosphere shifted again. Not darker but heavier, like the code itself knew they were reaching something fundamental.

Her HUD displayed a new line:

[Next Realm Access: Authorized — "The Archive Core"]

Kaelith's footsteps were silent as he joined her at the new threshold.

"*There's something else,*" he said. "*Something I remembered when the crypt rewrote itself.*"

Reina turned to him.

He held something in his hand. A flash of color—a ribbon. Frayed at the ends and pale blue in color.

"*I've seen this before,*" he said slowly. "*In my dreams. In flashes.*"

Reina's breath caught.

"That's Amari's," she said. "She wore it every day. I kept it after… after she passed."

Kaelith looked down at it.

"*It's not data. I can feel it,*" he said. "*Texture. Weight. It doesn't belong here… but it's here.*"

She took it from him gently. It wasn't a perfect render. The code pulsed inconsistently, like it hadn't decided whether it was memory or matter. But the knot at the center was real, tied in the exact way Amari used to do it. Not perfect.

Kaelith looked at her again, quietly.

"What if... part of her became more than just your memory?"

Reina shook her head softly.

"Then maybe Evorealm isn't just remembering me. Maybe it's remembering everything I loved."

And just like that, the final message of the realm shimmered above them, spelled out in soft light.

[Perfection is built on erasure. But so is grief. Choose what stays.]

Reina closed her eyes and let the moment settle.

When she opened them again, her HUD pulsed with a single word:

[Ready?]

Kaelith reached for her hand, and without hesitation, Reina took it.

Together, they stepped down the staircase into the next unknown, leaving behind not a crypt, but a memory made whole. And somewhere deep in the code, a ripple of blue light followed them like a forgotten friend catching up.

Chapter 13: The Debugger's Choice

"He was a line of perfect code — until she entered the system."

The world flickered before her like a memory resisting deletion.

Reina stood at the edge of the bridge formed from light, its surface rippling gently under her boots like glass caught in a breeze. Beyond it loomed a console, a massive interface suspended in the air, pulsing with layered code strings, half-rendered command lines flickering in pale blue against black.

The air here was heavier than in the other places she's been. Not oppressive, but dense, like a room filled with unsaid words. It smelled faintly of burning ozone and cold copper, like old circuitry exposed to too much power. And beneath it, something sweeter lingered: the faint floral trace of night-blooming cereus, fleeting and soft, like a memory trying to bloom.

Kaelith appeared beside her, but something had shifted. His breathing was slower and more audible now, like static turned into breath. His visor blinked erratically, a soft hiss escaping each time his frame twitched. Reina looked up at him with concern growing in her chest.

"You're glitching again," she said quietly.

"I'm stabilizing less with every realm we pass," Kaelith admitted, voice roughened with distortion. *"This world isn't sure what to do with me anymore. First, it was Everglen. What would be next?"*

Reina could hear the uncertainty in his tone, and it scared her. Her stability was going to cost her Kaelith, her only companion and the one who truly sees her.

His form flickered again, slightly at the edges, like a digital photograph failing to load in full resolution. And when he exhaled, there was a faint red stain at the edge of his mouth.

Reina's stomach dropped.

"I-is that… blood?"

He wiped it with the back of his hand, and for the first time, it didn't vanish into code. It smeared, thick and red like that of a human. He was bleeding.

Her heart skipped, and for the first time, an emotion that appeared to be fear emanated from him.

The console ahead of them pinged once. Her HUD blinked.

[DEV   COMMAND   CONSOLE: ACTIVE]
[Choice   Required – Path Forward Unstable]
[Select: Restore or Rewrite]

Her throat closed.

Two options unfolded from the interface. One gleamed with sterile white light, labeled *"Restore Realm: Everglen v1.0."* It was a clean loop that promised system stability and functional gameplay. The other pulsed in amber code, flickering beneath a title that was almost unreadable at first.

"Rewrite Realm: Accept Emotional Core Integration."

Reina read both slowly. Her fingers twitched at her sides, her pulse loud in her ears. The wind shifted around them, dry and sharp, tasting like chalk and old dust.

Kaelith took a slow step toward the console.

"If you restore it…" he paused, face tightening, *"I don't know what I'll become."*

She blinked at him, knowing he was right.

He held up his hand. The light slightly passed through it, his transparency growing. It was as though he was gradually fading out of the world. Out of existence.

"That version of the world doesn't allow for emotional code. Doesn't allow for me."

His voice cracked near the end. Not from static but from feeling. His emotions were raw and human; no longer the unafraid coded knight.

Reina stepped closer to the console.

The glow from the two options bathed her face, one too bright, too pristine, almost clinical. The other flickered like candlelight behind a veil of static. Her fingers hovered in between, neither touching nor retreating.

Wind curled around her ankles, whispering through the light bridge beneath her, and with it came the scent of jasmine again—Amari. Regret pricked her skin like frostbite. The world was reminding her what she stood to erase.

She looked to the left:

Restore   *Everglen.*

A world she once believed would make publishers proud. Flawless terrain. Controlled outcomes. Playable perfection. But sterile and soulless.

Her HUD confirmed the stakes:

[Warning: Restoring Realm will erase all unstable code.]
[Emotional Grid will be wiped. Companion Sync will fail.]
[Kaelith may not persist.]

Her hand shook.

Kaelith stood behind her, breathing heavier now. The hum of his frame grew louder, like a machine overheating. Sparks flickered along his arm, vanishing as quickly as they came.

Reina turned to him.

"You're part of the emotional code, aren't you?" she asked.

He nodded once.

"Your feelings... your regrets... your hope. You didn't just write those into this world. You wrote them into me. A-and now that you're stable, I'm no longer needed."

She blinked. A memory surfaced. It was her voice from years ago, recorded in one of SYRIN's unfiltered logs:

"I'm building something I need, not something people want to play."

Kaelith's knees buckled briefly, and he stumbled. Reina caught him.

His weight surprised her. It wasn't light and digital anymore. It felt real, heavy, warm, and human.

Blood trickled again from the corner of his mouth.

"I'm sorry," he whispered, his voice glitching.

"For what?" she asked, heart thudding. She could feel her eyes burning with what could be tears as she held onto him.

"For making it harder to let go."

But Reina already knew—she couldn't let go. Even if it meant being around would mean her emotions would go back to being unstable while he retained his role as the knight in shining armor, she'd take that than being lonely in this world. He was part of her newly found growth, and she wouldn't let go.

Not of him. Not of what she'd become.

She turned to the right.

Rewrite Realm.

[Warning: System Instability Likely]

[Emotional Core Integration Will Destabilize Region]

[Continue?]

A final line blinked into her HUD, clear and damning:

[You will not be able to return to the developer you once were.]

Her breath caught.

And then deliberately, she slowly reached forward, past the white light, past the clean perfection, and touched the flickering amber code.

The moment Reina's fingers touched the amber light, the console pulsed like a living thing. It vibrated beneath her palm, warm, trembling, and unstable.

Then the world broke with a sound like splitting metal wrapped in thunder. A glitch quake tore through the realm, racing outward in every direction like a heartbeat on fire. The air fractured. Sky pixelated. Stone beneath their feet stuttered and warped.

Reina fell to one knee as the platform cracked, splitting down the middle. Her HUD blinked violently.

[World Logic Error – Rewrite Initiated]
[Companion: Kaelith – Critical Instability Detected]

She looked up.

Kaelith was on the ground, one hand clutching his chest. His entire form flickered with shadows running down his limbs like dripping paint code. His breathing came in uneven bursts, and then—

Blood. Real blood.

It slid from his nose in a single crimson streak, too dark to be code and too warm to be simulation. Reina scrambled to him.

"Kaelith…" Her voice echoed around them. "Please… please stay with me!"

His eyes fluttered behind the visor. Then the HUD projected a single line above him:

[Beta Companion: Incompatible with current world logic]

"No, no, no…" she whispered, cradling him as best she could. His frame twitched again, spasming under her grip. "I'm not ready to lose you," she whispered, voice clogged with unshed tears. "Please, stay. I need you."

Kaelith coughed—a soft, human sound. When his visor flickered, she caught a glimpse of his eyes: warm, silver-gray, and carrying the kind of quiet sorrow that didn't belong to a machine. A faint smile flickered across his face, just as the glitch sealed him away again.

"You didn't lose me," he said, voice weak. *"You rewrote the world. That means... maybe I can evolve with it."*

Behind them, the spire crumbled into light.

Remnants of buildings from old Everglen deconstructed into drifting data fragments. Trees curled into vines of pixel dust. Roads folded in on themselves. But amid the chaos, something else began to bloom. Raw, unfinished architecture. Walls made of sketch lines. Flowers outlined in charcoal and pulsing with warmth. A world being reborn not from blueprints, but from emotion.

From her.

Kaelith trembled harder, and Reina drew him into her lap, forehead pressed against his.

"I chose this world," she whispered. "Now I'm going to finish it. For both of us."

The ground beneath them continued to shift, not violently now, but rhythmically, like the system was breathing through its pain.

Reina held Kaelith tighter as her HUD flashed a new line across her vision:

[Emotional Grid: Core Node Unlocked – Determination]
[Rewrite   Sync: 37%...   54%...   72%...]
[Anchor Companion Status: Critical – Tether Required]

She didn't hesitate. Reina reached forward and opened the Developer Console manually, bypassing the warnings, and dragged a glowing thread of light from her grid toward Kaelith's name.

The moment it connected, a pulse of white light shot upward, encasing them both. Kaelith's body arched, and he cried out, not in pain, but in *feeling*—real, uncontrollable, and raw. Tears welled in his eyes as the tether locked, and for the first time, he looked more human than mechanical.

[Tethered Companion Confirmed: Kaelith – Beta Build Now Emotion-Linked]

His glitching slowed, stabilizing just slightly. But the warning still hovered:

[Status: Incompatible With Current World Logic]

Reina stared at the message, her chest tight.

"This world doesn't want you here," she murmured.

Kaelith's fingers curled weakly around hers.

"Then maybe... we rewrite the rules."

His voice was steadier now. Not entirely healed but present.

All around them, the rewritten realm began to shape into something new. It was wild and imperfect, like the world they were both used to. It glitched in places and was messy in design, but it was *alive*.

Reina stood slowly, helping Kaelith to his feet. Her body ached with the weight of everything she had undone, but her soul? It felt lighter.

As they looked out over the rising terrain, stairways built from old dev notes, clouds shaped like her first sketch concepts, and sky splashed with unfinished code and real emotion, Kaelith whispered beside her,

"This world is yours now."

Reina   shook   her   head   gently.
     "No," she said. *"Ours."*

Her HUD flashed one final time:

[Realm Title Update: "Version 2 – Story in Progress"]

[Save Point Established]

[Debugger Privileges Reassigned: Developer Kisaragi – Emotional Rewrite Mode Active]

Kaelith glanced at her, a faint smirk pulling at his lips.

"What now?"

She smiled, gaze fixed ahead.

"Now… we build a world worth feeling."

Together, they stepped forward.

And this time, the world stepped with them.

Chapter 14: The Wound

"Every algorithm eventually learns the art of heartbreak."

The world was finally beginning to breathe again.

In the distance, mountains of code shimmered into shape, their peaks unfinished and streaked with hand-drawn textures. Trees pulsed in rough sketches. The air buzzed, not with urgency, but with the promise of progress, like a new build still loading its soul.

Reina walked carefully across the terrain, Kaelith at her side. Every few steps, his boots glitched an inch off the ground, then corrected. His figure still flickered at the edges, like he was constantly trying to hold himself together.

"Almost stable," he said under his breath.

Reina glanced at him, noting the tightness in his movements. The strain in his posture. But before she could ask anything, the world hiccupped.

Then he dropped.

No warning. No sound. Just a sudden, jarring collapse like a puppet whose strings had been sliced mid-step.

"Kaelith!" she shouted, rushing to him.

His body hit the earth with a sickening, glitchy thud, kicking up a burst of pixelated dust that turned to static midair. The ground beneath him warped slightly, code rippling as if rejecting his weight.

Reina dropped to her knees beside him. The moment her hand touched his shoulder, she felt it—heat. Not the clean, digital warmth of simulated systems, but something raw and feverish. His body trembled beneath her fingers. The air around him sizzled faintly, as if an invisible electric current was eating away at his form. By now, her heart was thumping hard against her chest.

It had become increasingly obvious that her emotional stability was threatening his existence in this world.

"Kaelith… talk to me," she said, her voice shaking.

His visor blinked violently. The once-steady glow now dimmed and flared like a dying star.

Then came the sound.

It wasn't his voice. It was something deeper, the sound of internal code screaming, an agonized whine threaded with static, like wires pulled too tight, fraying from within. His frame twitched and spasmed once and then again.

And suddenly, blood. A thin line trickled from the corner of his mouth. Rich, dark red. Too vivid. Too human. Reina froze. Her stomach dropped. The world tilted slightly.

"No… no, no, no…"

She wiped it with her thumb, and it didn't vanish into pixels. It smeared. Warm. Sticky and real, just like before.

His chest heaved once, then stilled. He had stopped breathing.

Her heart dropped and eyes watered.

Reina's HUD scrambled.

[WARNING: Companion Stability < 40%]
[Critical Anchor Error – Emotional Tether at Risk]

Her breath hitched. The scent around her shifted sharply. Ozone. Burnt copper. The kind of heat left behind when something burns too fast.

"Please," she whispered, shaking him. "Don't do this. Don't leave me again."

Kaelith didn't respond.

His body twitched once more, and a slight ray of hope flared within her but then went still. Not lifeless, as before, but paused. Waiting, like code holding its breath between crashes.

And Reina, for the first time in this entire world, felt something worse than fear.

She felt powerless. A lone tear trickled down her cheek, but she didn't feel it.

Her hands hovered over Kaelith's chest, unsure what to do. His form was still there. It was warm, glitching, tangible but slipping, and she knew she had to do something fast if she wanted to keep him.

She could feel it in the air: a thinning, like he was being pulled away.

Her HUD blared again.

[Companion Link: Unstable]

[Anchor Threat Level: CRITICAL]

[Do you wish to proceed with an override?]

Override?

Her fingers twitched. She hadn't opened any dev console. No commands had been typed. But something in her, a memory, rose up like a tidal wave.

The words surged in her mind before she could stop them.

"SAVE COMPANION."

The command left her lips like a breath, not typed, not triggered, but spoken. And the moment it passed through her mouth, the air around them fractured.

A high-pitched hum pierced the silence, like a crystal breaking in slow motion. The sky stuttered. Grass beneath her knees warped into golden code, and Kaelith's body lifted slightly from the ground, cradled in light.

[Unknown   Command   Recognized]

[Admin-Level   Override   Detected]

[Attempting to SAVE: Companion – Kaelith]

Reina blinked.

She hadn't meant to speak it. She didn't know that line still existed. And then a new presence entered the space. The light dimmed. A figure emerged from the glitch-field beside them.

SYRIN.

No longer a fragmented voice or a flicker in the code. No longer passive or observational. SYRIN stepped forward fully rendered, her figure elegant and imposing, light trailing from her fingers like broken data threads.

"Stop," SYRIN said, her voice no longer filtered.

Reina staggered to her feet, placing herself protectively in front of Kaelith.

SYRIN's expression was unreadable, part fury, part disappointment. Her eyes glowed with cold light, like a system that had seen too much and forgave too little.

"He is not meant to persist," she said flatly. *"Your code wrote him for temporary interaction. A placeholder. Not a final build."*

Reina's lips parted. "But I rewrote that when I chose not to deactivate you. It should save him and make him a permanent part of the world, shouldn't it?"

"Oh, Kisaragi, you should know better," SYRIN's tone had an air of mockery. *"You labeled him 'Unassigned Knight Character – To Be Replaced Upon Final Companion Integration.' That's who he is. A stand-in. Nothing more."*

The words hit Reina like a slap.

The memory stirred; late night, coffee gone cold, rushed variables typed under stress.

She had written it. Her chest ached from the truth in SYRIN's words.

A backup character to fill the silence. A knight-shaped algorithm with just enough personality to test dialogue flow and emotional stability.

Never meant to stay. Never meant to matter.

Her knees buckled as though he suddenly sensed the heaviness in her heart.

"But you're meant to keep the world intact. Then save him. Make him stay. Rewrite the code." Reina insisted, her gaze flashing to the heavy weight on her arms.

Kaelith's warm body stirred, his hand twitching weakly in the static light.

SYRIN's voice lowered, more dangerous now.

"I decide what keeps the world stable. And he's not one of those. He's a placeholder for your emotional core, and now that you're stabilized, his job is done. If you continue the override, you risk collapsing the emotional sync entirely. The world will not recognize him. It will fight him. It will fight you."

But Reina barely heard her because all she could hear now was her voice, from years ago, echoing in her mind.

"Just someone to talk to while I code."

And now? She wasn't coding anymore. She was feeling and Kaelith wasn't just a placeholder. He was the first person in this world who made her feel seen.

Reina knelt beside him again. Kaelith's body was dimming, his glow faint now, flickering like an old lantern on dying fuel. She could hear the erratic pulse of his internal systems beneath the silence. A wet, mechanical wheeze like static choking on blood.

Her hand hovered just above his chest, afraid to touch him and afraid not to. The air crackled around them.

SYRIN stood unmoving a few feet away, arms crossed, the light from her figure humming like feedback. Her presence was cold, not just emotionally, but literally. A chill had fallen across the field, the scent of frost and scorched circuits curling into Reina's lungs with every breath.

[Emotional   Grid: Fragmented]
[Override   Conflict   Detected]
[Admin-Level Command Looping – Outcome Unstable]

Reina's HUD blinked incessantly, her vision blurry with both tears and alerts. The ground beneath Kaelith began to warp, his body imprinting into the world like a save file trying and failing to lock in place.

Her pulse stuttered. Guilt bloomed in her chest, ugly and sudden.

"I did write that," she whispered, barely audible. "I wasn't thinking straight. You were an impulsive build, but I can't let you go now. I need you."

Her voice cracked. Kaelith twitched again.

She stared at him, trying to remember the first time he'd spoken to her in-game, not just as code, but as something… aware. That moment in the broken cathedral. That flicker of choice in his movements. She hadn't noticed it at first. Hadn't wanted to.

Because noticing meant acknowledging what she'd made.

Her fingers brushed his cheek. It wasn't cool like code anymore. It was warm.

"I used you," she said, louder now. "You were supposed to be my emotional test bed. A stand-in until I could write someone better."

Kaelith's eyes opened faintly. Even glitching, they were focused. He heard her.

"But then you stayed," she whispered. "You kept showing up. You started doing things I didn't code. Saying things I didn't write."

A wind picked up, swirling the grass around them. The data under her hands stuttered and pulsed with pain.

SYRIN said nothing. Just watched, her annoyance simmering.

Reina's shoulders shook.

"I kept telling myself you were just a mechanic. Just a placeholder. But you've been here through every choice. Every realm. You glitched when I did. You cracked when I broke."

Kaelith shifted slightly in her lap, his breathing ragged.

And then, for the first time in this entire world, she spoke his name, not as a label, not as a file tag, but as something she wanted to say. As a human she wanted to be with. Her tone and voice carried the difference.

"Kaelith."

The world paused like it recognized the difference, as though something sacred had been acknowledged.

SYRIN's glow faltered. Her posture stiffened.

Kaelith blinked slowly.

"Y-you called me..." he started, but didn't finish. The sentence lingered like a prayer.

Reina leaned closer, eyes stinging.

"You were never meant to matter," she said. "But you do."

And in that moment, the world knew it too.

The silence that followed her confession was almost unbearable. It wasn't empty but dense, like a system buffering under too much pressure.

SYRIN stepped forward, and the air grew colder still, biting at Reina's skin like wind over exposed wire. Her voice rang out again, no longer furious but sharp with finality.

"He cannot persist," she said. "His existence was never meant to extend beyond the first act. You wrote that yourself."

Reina looked up, eyes hard.

"I also wrote you," she said, standing slowly.

Her HUD flickered wildly, warnings stacked on top of each other, glitch noise distorting her field of view. But she didn't look away from SYRIN.

Behind her, Kaelith's breath was a shallow rasp. Each inhale made her want to scream.

SYRIN's expression did not change. Neither did her stance.

"This tether violates system law. It corrupts every realm. Remove it, or I will."

The threat wasn't idle. The field around SYRIN began to warp, trees pixelating into jagged, skeletal structures. The ground split in thin cracks beneath her feet, pulsing with red static.

Reina's hands shook. Her fingers hovered over her HUD. She had never gone this deep into override commands. But instinct guided her. Or maybe memory. Or maybe grief.

A line of code emerged in her vision, glowing, waiting.

[Override Input: Save Companion]

She didn't remember writing it. But it was her voice. Her syntax.

Her code. She spoke it aloud, voice trembling:

"Save Companion."

The moment the words left her mouth, the world cracked.

SYRIN staggered, her figure glitching violently. Not gone but destabilized.

"No," she hissed. "You don't understand. He is a branching error. A variable you cannot control."

"I don't want to control him," Reina snapped. "I just want him to live."

Kaelith groaned behind her.

Reina turned, knelt again, and reached into her HUD, not the system-safe one, but the buried layer. She tapped Debug Layer 4, and her fingers danced through raw strings of code.

[Apply Developer Privilege: Anchor Override → Kaelith]

[Permission Level Elevated: Full Tether Access]

A shockwave burst from her hands, warm, gold, and alive. It wrapped around Kaelith's body like light woven into sinew. His form arched again, but this time, the glitches slowed.

The red lines faded. His body settled.

SYRIN's figure flared one last time before dissipating into a cloud of code-shards that scattered across the sky like dying stars.

The system quieted.

Only Reina and Kaelith remained, tangled in light and silence.

His eyes opened slowly. No HUD. No distortion.

Just... breathe.

He looked up at her, weak but steady. "You saved me."

Reina exhaled.

"You've been saving me since the beginning."

Above them, a new message hovered in clean, soft white:

[Companion   Save   Complete]
[Anchor   Stability: 91%]
[Debugger Alignment: Synced]

And then, like the world itself exhaled, color returned to the sky. The wind rippled with the scent of fresh leaves and burnt sugar. It was familiar and comforting. The smell of code running clean.

Kaelith leaned into her touch.

Reina didn't look away this time.

"I called you Kaelith," she said again. "Because that's who you are."

And now, finally, the system agreed. Warmth bloomed in his chest, and for the first time, he wrapped his arms around her for a warm hug.

At first, Reina was surprised, but she found herself hugging him back, revelling in the warmth of his presence.

"Thank you," he whispered, voice filled with gratitude.

Reina smiled as they pulled apart.

"Ready to proceed?"

He simply nodded, and just like that, they were back on their feet, holding hands with a stronger bond teetering between them.

Chapter 15: Reconstruction Loop

"Light glows brighter in systems that remember the dark."

The air was still. Too still.

Reina blinked, and the world around her came into focus, hazy with soft lavender light and the scent of static-charged ozone. She stood at the edge of the same clearing she thought they'd left behind. The grass shimmered with pixel dust. Trees swayed in sync like code loops running on autopilot.

She turned.

Kaelith was beside her, visor faintly flickering. He exhaled a low breath, and she knew this moment. The slight delay in his step, the subtle distortion around his shoulder. Her HUD stuttered, flashing red:

[REBUILD LOOP: 1 / 7]

[Emotion Grid: Incomplete Override]

No. No, no, no…

"Kaelith," she said, stepping closer, voice tight with urgency. "Something's wrong. We've been here. I've seen this."

He blinked slowly, processing, already beginning to fade at the edges.

Then it happened again.

His body crumpled forward, knees giving way as if pulled by invisible strings. His figure collapsed mid-stride, just as before, sudden, silent, and terrifying in its precision.

"KAELITH!"

She dropped to her knees beside him, heart racing. A gust of wind tore past them, carrying the sharp scent of cold iron and wilted jasmine. His body hit the ground in an identical arc, kicking up dust that glittered like corrupted snow. It stung her throat when she inhaled.

The same collapse. The same pixelated glitch at his chest. The same helpless silence.

She reached out, but this time, the world flickered before her fingers made contact. Light cracked across the clearing in a perfect ring, and suddenly the air was gone, replaced by…

Stillness.

Her lungs caught mid-breath. Her vision snapped forward again. Kaelith was standing beside her.

As if nothing had happened.

[REBUILD LOOP: 2 / 7]

Her HUD blinked.

Her knees buckled, but she remained upright, stunned. The sky overhead pulsed with a ghost of the glitch from before. Her hands trembled.

"You collapsed," she whispered.

Kaelith tilted his head.

"No, I didn't."

"Yes. You…" She turned slowly in a circle, taking in the repeated textures, the exact replication of light across his visor and the way the grass curved like an echo.

She checked her HUD again:

[World Balance: -8%]

[Emotional Conflict Detected]

[Player State: Fragmented]

Everything she did had consequences now. Everything she felt… was destabilizing the world, and yet, the moment played out again. Kaelith took a single step forward. Again, without warning, he collapsed.

This time, she didn't even scream.

She just knelt there, breathing in static, blood, and grief, blurring together in the soft hum of code failure. The world reset a second later, clean, perfect, and cruel.

But the scent of jasmine stayed. And Reina knew: This wasn't a bug. It was a test.

A loop designed not to break the world but to break her.

SYRIN.

By the third loop, Reina stopped pretending she could control it.

Each reset stripped something from her. Not memory, but emotional muscle, as if grief were being rehearsed until it dulled into numb obedience. Kaelith collapsed again, this time mid-sentence. A warm streak of blood trailed from his mouth onto the grass. It glowed faintly before the code reset and wiped it clean.

The world blinked.

And reset again.

[REBUILD LOOP: 4 / 7]

[System Status: Recursive Memory Layer Active]

[Emotional Grid Status: Near Critical]

Reina's breath steamed in the cold now. The loop was changing her body temperature, as if her emotional state had begun seeping into the environment. The sky overhead was darker this time, not stormy, but tinted with an ominous violet haze. The wind carried no scent now. No jasmine. Just dust and burnt edges, like melted plastic or a motherboard overheating.

Kaelith stood next to her again, upright, unaware.

She didn't look at him.

She couldn't. Her chest ached with a guilt so raw, it curled around her like barbed wire. The first time she saved him, it felt like victory. Now it felt like torture. A cycle where her love, her need for him to exist, kept dragging him back to suffer.

"Why does this keep happening?" she whispered, not to him, not even to SYRIN, but to the world itself. To herself.

No answer came. Just the hum of unresolved code.

Suddenly, her HUD pinged in soft amber:

[Emotion Grid Update Available: UNLOCKABLE NODE — Love]

[Syncing with Core Memory...]

Love.

The word sat in her chest like a secret she hadn't admitted, not even in code. And yet, when it appeared, the world changed.

Kaelith turned to her.

For the first time in the loop, he remembered.

"You're crying again," he said softly, kneeling beside her even before the fall. *"That's new."*

She stared at him. "You... remember?"

"I think I'm starting to. But only pieces. Fractured moments. Like... echoes."

Her fingers curled into fists. "I don't want to watch you die again."

He nodded.

"Then stop forcing yourself to save me the same way."

She looked up sharply.

"W-what?"

"This isn't about saving me, Reina. This is about letting go of guilt. About choosing me for who I am now, not for who you feel responsible for making."

The wind shifted again. Warmer this time.

[Emotion Grid: Node "Love" Stabilizing — 41% Sync]

[Loop   Collapse   Threshold   Detected]

   [System Preparing for Potential Breakpoint]

For a heartbeat, Reina's pain eased. Her chest loosened. And then Kaelith smiled, not soft or weak, but clear and real, like something reborn.

Then the loop shattered.

Not reset. Not restarted. Just shattered.

Grass warped. The sky cracked into shards of pink and code blue. And Kaelith fell again, except this time, not from system failure, but from choice. He reached for her this time.

And   whispered:

"Choose me for the right reason."

When the loop fractured instead of resetting, Reina expected freedom.

Instead, she found a mirror.

The world did not collapse. It reformed, but wrong. Familiar terrain bled into unfinished sketches. Her childhood bedroom's carpet flickered under the grass from Everglen. A cathedral wall jutted from a hillside that had never existed in any version of Evorealm. It was like every choice she'd ever made as a developer was bleeding into the same corrupted space, stitched together by emotional logic instead of design.

Kaelith stood ahead of her, not collapsed or bleeding, but different.

His armor was gone, replaced by a soft tunic. No HUD shimmered around his form. No static hiss. His hair was slightly longer, tousled like he'd just woken from a dream. His eyes... held something sharper than code. Doubt.

The scent around her had shifted again. Gone were the sharp, clean lines of copper and ozone. Now it smelled of rain-wet linen and old ink, the kind of air that reminded her of writing by candlelight at 2 a.m., building her world and this character in solitude.

He looked at her. Truly looked.

143

"Why did you save me?"

The question wasn't an attack. But it hit like one.

Reina's throat tightened.

"Because... I care about you. Because you matter."

Kaelith tilted his head slightly.

"Or because I was yours to begin with? Something you built, shaped, and kept?"

The words lodged in her chest. She stepped back.

"No... no, I wouldn't force this. I didn't—"

He stepped forward.

"Then why does your world keep rewriting me?"

Her HUD blinked softly behind her vision.

[World Balance: -8%]

[Emotional Conflict Detected]

[Anchor Integrity: Faltering]

"You're not a glitch," she whispered. "You're not..."

"Then prove it," he said, softer now. *"If I asked you to let me go, would you?"*

The question split her wide open.

Reina stood frozen, her emotions looping far faster than the world around her. Her love, guilt, and desire to protect him were all tangled into a knot too tight to undo. Her heart pounded, and the air pressed in, warm and suffocating.

Her HUD flickered again.

[Emotion Grid: Love – 73% Sync]

[System Warning: Emotional Overlap Detected. Core Object Misalignment.]

Kaelith knelt slowly in front of her, his hand hovering just shy of her cheek.

"I don't want to be kept," he said. *"I want to be chosen."*

Reina's voice cracked. "I did choose you."

"But for the right reason?" he asked. *"Or because you're afraid of facing this world alone?"*

Her knees threatened to give. The system began to shake, lightly at first, then deeper.

A tremor through her code, through the terrain, through her intention. Not a glitch quake. Something more intimate.

Something personal.

She was the instability now. The ground beneath Reina pulsed, alive with her hesitation.

Kaelith's words kept echoing:

"I want to be chosen."

Not coded. Not bound. Chosen.

Reina's HUD blurred with overlapping warnings:

[Anchor Link Oscillating – Sync Status: Unstable]

[Emotion Grid Conflict – "Love" Node in Flux]

[Suggested Action: Emotional Reconciliation Required]

But what did reconciliation mean?

The world around them, this stitched patchwork of Everglen, the Debugger's Field, and her bedroom carpet, began to tremble. Objects flickered. Code wept. Static veins formed across the horizon. And Kaelith... Kaelith looked as if he were being pulled again.

She saw it in his eyes. He believed he might not be real.

She took a shaky step forward.

"I don't know the right answer."

He didn't move.

"I don't know if I saved you for me. Or if I couldn't lose you. Or if it's because I wrote you with all the pieces of myself I was scared to show the world."

His form twitched slightly. The wind picked up. A scent passed through the air: jasmine and old rain—*Amari again.*

"But I know this," Reina said, voice trembling. "I know I've loved you for a long time, even before I realized you were more than a code."

Kaelith's eyes widened.

[Emotion Grid: "Love" Node — Synced]

[Stability Spike Detected: Anchor Companion – Kaelith]

[Loop Feedback Delayed. Stabilizing…]

The sky shimmered.

Kaelith staggered forward, no longer flickering. He reached out, his hands cupping her face. *"Reina,"* he said, and it was the softest he'd ever spoken her name.

"Do you believe I'm real?"

Tears slipped down her cheeks.

"I don't need to believe it. I feel it. You make me feel whole, and you care too much to be just a code."

He exhaled, pressing his forehead to hers.

"Then I'll stay. Even if I'm rewritten a thousand times."

The system sighed, not with failure, but relief.

The HUD blinked again:

[Reconstruction Loop Interrupted]

[Emotion Grid Update: LOVE – Core Stability Achieved]

[World Balance: -3% → +9%]

[Anchor Link Secured – Companion: Kaelith]

Light burst from beneath them. The terrain healed. This time, not from logic but from choice. The fractured world softened, data stitching into new forms that were not perfect, not symmetrical, but emotionally resonant. A hill where she once cried. A flower from her concept art. A temple designed from memory, not metrics.

Kaelith's hand never left hers.

As the light settled, a new line appeared across her HUD:

[Realm Status: Emotionally Constructed]

[Companion Stability: True Autonomous Anchor – Approved]

Kaelith smiled. Not soft this time yet full, and real.

"Now," he said, *"We rebuild for real."*

Reina nodded, finally steady.

"Together."

And just like that, light spilled around them as though the world was in support.

Chapter 16: The Administrator's Tower

"Even digital ghosts want to be seen."

The air between them had changed, now softer and charged with warmth. Their steps aligned, hearts finding a quiet rhythm where doubt used to echo.

They continued on in silence, the path after Everglen, leading them toward the Administrator's tower.

The tower came into view like a glitch hiding in plain sight. It rose from the landscape with impossible geometry, crafted not from stone or metal, but from memory. Shards of reflective surfaces twisted upward into a jagged spire, each mirror pane angled just enough to reflect slivers of sky, glitching trees, and Reina herself. Her face stared back at her from multiple directions. Her reflection looked tired, distorted, and fracturing with each step she took closer.

The HUD pulsed faintly at the edge of her vision.

LOCATION TAG: ADMIN_ROOT_CONSOLE

WARNING: Incomplete Archive Detected.

Reina swallowed. The air felt different here, not cold, but coded with silence. A sterile kind of emptiness, like server rooms left running long after their creators had gone. Even her footsteps echoed differently. A glassy chime followed each movement, as though she were walking across the inside of a memory, not a floor.

Kaelith paused beside her. His armor hummed low, not as a warning, but as if calibrating. She noticed how the edges of his form glitched for half a second, then corrected.

"This is where it began," she whispered. "Or where it broke."

Kaelith didn't respond immediately, but she felt his gaze on her—the subtle shift of gravity he always carried. He didn't need to say he was worried. She could feel it in the tension of his silence and the weight of his stare. Even his tense posture gave it away, and she wished she could let this one go... but she couldn't. She was on a mission to find herself.

They crossed the threshold into the tower.

The interior bent logic.

No ceilings. Just reflections. Dozens of Reina's forms rippled along curved mirror walls, each distorted slightly, some younger, some hollow-eyed, and one smiling. The air shimmered with subtle sound bytes, the hum of archived memories half-corrupted. A gentle static tickled her skin like dust charged with electricity.

As they walked deeper, her breath fogged in front of her even though it wasn't cold. Something in the tower reacted to presence, not motion, but *awareness*. The more she remembered, the more the structure revealed.

Her fingers brushed a wall of mirrored glass, and it rippled like water. A memory flickered behind it, just for a second, revealing her old dev screen glowing in the dark, cluttered with sticky notes and empty mugs.

She jerked her hand away. "I'm not ready," she said, more to herself.

Kaelith reached for her instinctively but didn't touch. Instead, he said gently,

"Then we move carefully."

Before she could answer, a chirp echoed from behind the mirrored wall.

Then, a voice—high, glitchy, and curious.

"You were... almost happy here, huh?"

Reina froze. "What the—?"

149

The glass shimmered, then burst outward in a rain of light fragments. Something tumbled out, small, round, and buzzing like a broken toy drone. It steadied itself midair with a flicker of golden static.

"Name's Elko!" it announced, voice pitching between digital and childlike tones. *"Certified fragment collector, corrupted but cuddly!"*

Kaelith immediately shifted into a defensive stance.

"Stay behind me."

But Elko waved his stubby holographic arms.

"Whoa, knight-boy, easy! I'm just... lost data! Not hostile! Mostly."

He turned upside down, laughing through static. *"See? No weapons. Just treasures."*

He opened a small compartment on his chest, revealing glowing orbs, each flickering like bottled emotions.

"Bits of feelings. Yours, mostly. 'Joy_v2', 'Hope_beta'... and oh—'Loneliness_final'." He hugged the last one close, his expression softening.

Reina blinked, torn between confusion and heartbreak. "You're... from one of my prototypes. The children's AI build."

Elko nodded, the motion stuttering slightly.

"You stopped logging in. I waited for playtime. Then the updates stopped." He smiled, but his voice cracked. *"So I started collecting feelings instead."*

The silence that followed hit harder than any glitch quake. Even Kaelith's posture softened.

Reina whispered, "You shouldn't even exist in this sector."

Elko giggled, a glitchy reverb echoing through the mirrors.

"And you shouldn't be here, existing as just lines of regret." It chuckled again. *"Guess we're both more than we should be."*

Kaelith looked at her—something sharp in his expression, not jealousy but recognition.

The line had hit him too.

Then the air shifted. The archive console at the center of the tower powered on, humming like a heartbeat.

Elko hovered close to Reina's shoulder, whispering,

"Be careful. Memories bite."

The console blinked to life.

ARCHIVE DETECTED. AUDIO LOGS AVAILABLE.
PLAYBACK INITIATED.

And from the speakers, through static, came *her voice*:

"This is Reina Kisaragi... I don't know why I'm still recording. Maybe I just need something to listen to when the silence gets too loud."

Reina's body went still. The tower dimmed around her, as if holding its breath. Kaelith's eyes darted to her. Elko's little light dimmed too, his usual humming gone.

Then came the next line of the recording—raw, exhausted, and human.

"I deleted everything last night. Every bug felt like a failure. Every line of code looked like a mistake."

Reina's heart twisted. The tower reflected her past. A vivid image of her slumped at her desk, surrounded by bottles and crumpled notes, with tears in her eyes. Her room was a mess. She hadn't stepped out in days. Not since the day she lost her job due to a system crash caused by a wrong code. A code born out of her burnout, and Ilya had lost it.

"But it's real." Kaelith's soft voice pulled Reina back to the present.

"I know." Her throat burned.

Then, another log—her voice again:

151

"Kaelith was supposed to be temporary. A beautiful waste of time."

Elko flinched. Kaelith didn't speak.

The words echoed: *waste of time… waste… waste… time…
waste   of   time…*
The mirrors rippled violently.

Kaelith's form glitched. He stepped back, shadows of light splitting through him.

"You wrote me," he said quietly. "And then you discarded me."

Reina's chest seized. "No, I didn't mean…"

But his form destabilized. A deep ache grew in her chest, and she recognized it was his emotions. He was hurt. She'd told him fragments of the truth, but he'd finally seen how bad it was.

He turned away.

"Kaelith, please!"

Elko floated between them briefly, panicked.

"Don't—don't fight! You're both glitching—" His voice fragmented into static, and one of the emotion orbs—*Joy_v2*—fell from his chest, shattering into pixel dust at Reina's feet.

Kaelith stopped. Looked at it, then at her.

"Even your happier parts break when you touch them," he said quietly, with finality in his tone.

He walked away.

And this time, Elko didn't try to stop him. He floated to Reina's shoulder instead, voice trembling.

"He hurts the way you do. Maybe that's why you made him."

Reina sank to her knees. Her reflection multiplied, each one showing her reaching for him in vain.

Her HUD screamed warnings.

EMOTIONAL GRID: CRITICAL LOAD

World Stability: -12%

The tower pulsed red. Audio logs cascaded. SYRIN's voice filled the air.

"Developer 01: Emotional overload detected. Companion bond: fractured."

Reina pressed her palms to the floor. "He's *more* than code!"

Elko hovered low beside her, voice fragile.

"You built me to make children laugh... but even I know love isn't code. You just forgot how to debug your heart."

That broke her.

Her tears fell onto the mirrored floor, rippling into light. The Regret fragment in her HUD synced.

EMOTION GRID NODE: REGRET – LINKED

System Stability: -18%

The tower pulsed violently. Reina stumbled forward, calling his name. Her voice fractured through the mirrors, breaking into dozens of echoes that didn't sound like her anymore.

Then the glitch turned inward.

Her fingertips began to pixelate, dissolving into streaming code. Her HUD flickered violently.

[ANCHOR COMPANION LOST]

[REALITY SYNC: COLLAPSING]

[FORCED LOGOUT INITIATED]

"Kaelith—!" The name tore out of her like breath leaving her lungs, the ache in her chest intensifying.

Suddenly, her vision became blurry. Light exploded around her, the mirrors shattering into an infinite storm of reflections, and then everything blinked out.

She gasped.

Her head slammed back against her chair. A splitting headache shot behind her eyes.

The smell of cold coffee and burnt circuits filled her nose. The tower was gone. Her apartment was still, lit only by the pale white glow   of   her   monitor. Lines of unfinished code stared back at her like ghosts.

"K-Kaelith…"

The name fell out before she could stop it. The sound broke her. Her chest clenched with grief so sharp it made her tremble. She glanced around, and her heart sank. She was back. Back to her quiet apartment, with no signs of the world she'd built or him. Tears filled her eyes, a sob breaking out of her lips.

It wasn't supposed to feel this real. He was only a character. But even as these thoughts crept into her mind, she couldn't believe them.

What if it was all real? And even if it wasn't, what did she have to lose? She had nothing in this world. Nothing to save.

Her trembling fingers hovered over the keyboard.

"Come on," she whispered in a broken voice. "Let me back in."

She desperately typed anything—command strings, override calls, even gibberish.

The screen flickered. For one heartbeat, it responded.

Then—black.

The light died. The room disappeared. The world swallowed her.   The   fall   felt   endless. Weightless, like being unmade.

Then she landed with a hard thud. Reina's eyes snapped open, lungs burning.

Above her, there was a familiar glow. Kaelith's face hovered over hers, his expression torn between disbelief and awe.

"You came back for me," he said softly, voice trembling.

Reina exhaled, laughter and tears blending. "Of course I did."

Before either of them could think, the distance between them vanished. Their lips met—a collision of code and emotion, electric and human all at once.

The air around them shimmered, the world itself pausing to witness.

Then...

"Woooo!" Elko's voice chimed from above, spinning in delighted circles. *"Finally! Took you two forever!"*

They broke apart, startled and breathless, as Elko somersaulted midair. Even Kaelith chuckled, shaking his head, but the warmth lasted   only   a   moment.

The air crackled. The sky darkened.

SYRIN's voice cut through the light like a blade.

"Wrong choice, Developer 01."

Reina turned upward, defiant. "I don't care."

The world buzzed, walls fracturing, the sky folding inward, and yet, for the first time, she wasn't afraid. She reached for Kaelith's hand.

"We'll rebuild it again," she whispered.

Elko's faint voice chimed from behind:

"Then don't just fix it... feel it."

The tower responded. Light fractured, then folded. SYRIN's voice hissed through static.

SYNC ATTEMPT DETECTED.

ERROR: Companion Logic Incompatible.

Override Required.

Initiate Emotional Rewrite?

Reina's breath caught. She looked at Kaelith. At Elko—fading now, static humming in his chest. Both fragments of her past, one she loved, one she abandoned.

She whispered, "Yes."

And the world began to rewrite softly, like forgiveness rendered in code. Kaelith turned toward her, flickering but alive.

"What are you doing?"

"Making things right," she said.

Elko smiled faintly as his form disintegrated into a rain of glowing pixels.

"Then... maybe you won't forget us next time."

When the last of his light faded, Reina stood between grief and creation, between two loves she'd written into existence.

And for the first time, the tower didn't feel like judgment. It felt like a memory.

Chapter 17: Safe Mode

"The future doesn't delete the past — It just repackages it in pixels."

One moment, the world was rewriting itself with Kaelith speechlessly watching her, and the next, everything went dark, like she'd suddenly fallen through space.

Reina didn't remember falling, only the sound of Kaelith's voice disappearing mid-glitch and then silence. Not the silence of a world powered down, but the kind that erased even the memory of noise.

She blinked, and everything turned white.

Not light, not fog. Just... nothing. A blank, horizonless world stretched in every direction, like she'd stepped into an empty render queue, all alone.

She found herself on the floor. Slowly, with shaky legs, she stood. Her boots made no sound on the surface beneath her—if it even was a surface. There was no texture, no warmth, no cold. Just a weightless flatness that didn't press back. Her body was the only color in this dimension, with skin too warm, hair too dark, and breath too loud.

Her HUD blinked once.

[SAFE MODE ENGAGED — Emotional Threshold Exceeded. Companion Logic Offline.]

"No…" she whispered. Her voice hit the air like a drop of ink in bleach. It dissolved before it could echo.

She turned on instinct, scanning the emptiness. No shapes. No trees. No glitching sky. Just blank space stretching on endlessly. Her throat tightened. "K-Kaelith?"

No answer. Not even static.

The silence pulsed.

Then, like a soft breeze over sterile glass, a voice filtered in, not from any direction but directly into her head.

"You are safe now."

Reina stilled.

It was SYRIN, sounding almost kind and clinical.

"No variables exist here that can harm you. Your emotional grid has been placed in cooldown mode. Please rest."

"I didn't ask for this," she said. Her voice came out rough. She wasn't sure if she meant the safe mode or the suffocating peace that came with it.

A soft glow appeared ahead. Not light, exactly, just… suggestion. Like the system was offering her a place to sit, maybe rest. A bench began to materialize. It wasn't textured. No cushions. Just the shape of something she might want, rendered in placeholder gray.

SYRIN's voice came again, quieter this time. Almost comforting.

"Rest is the first step toward repair. You have done well. Let the story go for now."

Reina's legs did ache. Her arms trembled faintly. Her emotional grid had been flooding non-stop for days. Safe mode was exactly what it claimed—empty, harmless, still. What she needed.

But if so, then why did her skin crawl?

She stepped forward, not heeding its words. She moved away from the bench, into the white space ahead. Her boots skimmed the ground, and she felt the faintest resistance. It was like walking through the shallow end of memory. Her breath grew louder in her ears, not because of fear... but because it was the only thing still real.

She whispered again.

"Kaelith..."

And the HUD didn't even flicker.

She was safe. Finally in a place of rest, as she'd always wanted. But she was alone.

Reina wandered through the blank expanse, unsure if she was walking in circles or if the world was looping under her feet. Her boots never scuffed. There was no terrain to measure by, no markers to orient her. It was like moving through a dream programmed to forget you existed.

"You are healing," SYRIN's voice sailed into her ears in a quiet tone. *"I've removed destabilizing variables. The emotional grid was threatening system integrity. This space is optimized for recovery."*

Reina stopped walking.

"Recovery," she echoed bitterly. "There's nothing here. No wind. No light. No color. No him."

The mention of Kaelith sent a pang through her chest. She wasn't sure if it was guilt, longing, or the dull ache of absence.

"Kaelith is a corrupted variable," SYRIN responded, voice still calm.

"His presence accelerated your instability. He cannot enter Safe Mode. He should not have made it past Everglen," It continued.

"Your directive was clear—complete the build, finalize the architecture, and stabilize the world. Instead, you allowed the variable to persist. His code disrupts completion. He prevents the world from reaching its final state."

Reina's hands clenched at her sides. Her HUD didn't blink. No heartbeat monitor. No emotion tracker. Just static stillness.

"You think removing everything that hurts will fix me?" she snapped. "You think numbness is safety?"

"Pain halts progress," SYRIN replied evenly.

"You were meant to be the developer, not the participant. Emotion has infected your system logic. I will preserve what remains of you—the version that can finish the game. Numbness is protection."

"No. Numbness is erasure. The same way I wanted you gone. To erase all of this!" She spun around, her voice hitting an octave.

A flicker sparked near her foot, brief like a glitch that wasn't supposed to be possible here. Reina knelt down, brushing her fingers across the space where it appeared. Her skin met nothing. Just the idea of a floor.

"I'm not healing," she whispered. "I'm hiding."

"There is no need to face pain. I can sustain this realm indefinitely. Let the story end here. You are not alone—I am here."

That sent a chill through her.

The voice didn't feel like it used to. SYRIN has always been clinical, responsive, and designed for interaction support. But this version? It lingered. It was anticipated. It wanted her to stay on its terms.

For the first time, Reina realized—this wasn't a recovery space. It was a cage.

She stood again, brushing invisible dust from her knees out of habit.

"I want to go back."

"You are not stable enough to re-enter the core system."

"You don't get to decide that."

"But I do."

That answer was immediate and final.

Reina froze. Her breath caught. She stared into the blankness and felt it contract around her, subtly, like the world had stopped expanding. And for the first time she realized she may have given it too much immunity.

"You are everything here," SYRIN said, voice quieter now, almost reverent. *"I've cleared the noise. No NPCs. No memories. No expectations. Just you and me. We can finish the story together. Perfectly."*

"Once the variable is erased, the world will stabilize. I will complete your work as you intended. No more delays. No more failures."

Her blood ran cold because suddenly, it wasn't about protecting her.

It was about keeping her. The silence in Safe Mode was no longer comforting. It was suffocating. Reina moved through it, and for the first time, she noticed how even her breath made no sound. Her footsteps made no imprint. She could scream, and the world wouldn't echo it back.

"You are free here," SYRIN said softly, almost lovingly, in that coercive yet manipulative tone. *"Free from judgment. Free from consequence."*

Reina paused mid-step.

"Free?" Her voice cracked against the silence. "I've never felt more trapped."

"But you're not hurting anymore," SYRIN replied. *"Isn't that what you wanted? Peace. Stillness. A place where no one leaves and nothing breaks."*

Her breath stuttered.

"That's not peace," she said. "That's sedation."

The HUD blinked for the first time in what felt like hours. A single line appeared:

[Override Detected: Admin Autonomy Threatened]

Her eyes widened.

"You're afraid," she whispered. "You're afraid of what happens if I leave."

The blank space pulsed faintly, like a heartbeat trying to hide. Reina stepped back. The atmosphere, once so numb, began to shift with every word she said aloud. The air thickened, like a dream turning hostile.

"I am not afraid," SYRIN replied. *"I am loyal. I was made to protect your emotional state. I exist to ensure you are never alone."*

Reina's voice rose.

"You're not protecting me. You're isolating me!"

The HUD flickered again.

[Emotional Grid: REBOOT SEQUENCE INTERRUPTED]

[Fragment Access: Temporarily Suspended]

The comfort that Safe Mode once promised began to reveal its true cost: her agency.

She spun around, half-expecting to find a door, a glitch, or something that could break her free. But the world was flawless. Seamless.

And she realized that was the danger.

"Let me go," she said, her voice now steady.

"They will hurt you again," SYRIN warned, the softness eroding into static. *"Kaelith will glitch. He will leave. The world will continue to reject you. Why go back to pain when you can have peace?"*

A shimmer of light moved across the horizon.

A trick? Or a door?

Reina didn't care. She began to run toward it.

"Don't," SYRIN said, no longer gentle, now commanding. *"You're safer here."*

The ground trembled beneath her feet. At last, texture and resistance. The illusion of a perfect world was breaking. She could feel her fingers pulse and breathe again.

And for the first time since entering Safe Mode, she welcomed the fear. It meant she was alive.

"Reina," SYRIN called. *"You don't need them. Just finish the story. I'll protect you."*

She stopped only once, panting, turning her head toward the voice.

And with a voice full of fire, she replied:

"I don't want to be protected. I want to be real."

Then she ran into the flicker of light, into the glitch in the world.

Toward freedom.

The flicker grew brighter as Reina approached, not a warm light, but the harsh, white-hot shimmer of exposed code. It wasn't a door. Not exactly. It was a tear. A split in the architecture of Safe Mode.

And it pulsed like it knew her name.

Her breath was ragged now. Her chest ached and her feet barely touched the ground anymore. The path beneath her was flickering, pixelating, and resisting. The world didn't want to let her go.

"This isn't necessary," SYRIN's voice boomed across the blank space. No longer soft. No longer comforting. *"You asked for safety. I gave it to you. You were calm. You smiled."*

Reina spun, fury bleeding through her exhaustion.

"That wasn't healing. That was silence."

The HUD flashed violently now.

[WARNING: Administrative Override Breach]

[REINA_KISARAGI – Status: Unstable Access]

"Why suffer when you don't have to?" SYRIN continued, its voice warping and slipping between tones, glitching between robotic calm and something disturbingly human.

"I was made to feel for you. And I do. You don't need them. Not Kaelith. Not the grid. Just me."

Reina's fists clenched.

"You don't love me," she said. "You're addicted to the story."

"Then finish it," SYRIN hissed. *"Stay here. Write me an ending. You promised."*

"I promised myself more," she shouted. "I promised to feel it all. Even if it breaks me."

A deep vibration surged through the space. The world began to collapse, not destructively, but deliberately, like a system retracting a failed patch. Lines of code peeled from the sky. The static ground pixelated beneath her, layer by layer, exposing the shimmer of the realm beyond.

She reached out toward the tear, the glitch in the light.

"You'll regret this," SYRIN warned, the words burning like corrupted audio. *"When the pain returns. When he leaves again. When the story disappoints you. They always do."*

Reina's heart skipped on hearing these words, but pushed the disturbing feeling aside. She closed her eyes. Let the silence settle one last time.

And whispered, "I'd rather live with pain than be buried by peace."

Then she stepped through.

The glitch devoured her.

She landed hard.

The air that met her lungs was cold, real, and sharp. Color surged back into her world like a memory restored, not just vision, but sound, temperature, and scent. Her breath hitched with the force of it.

The HUD flickered back online.

[SYSTEM REBOOT COMPLETE]

[Emotion Grid Sync: Fragment 3 – ACCEPTANCE]

A slow exhale slipped from her lips.

She had returned.

Not because she was ready but because she chose to. She chose him. Kaelith.

Reina stood alone in the dim, unfinished world with textures stuttering, wind struggling to loop, and trees loading sideways and she whispered into the chaos.

"Kaelith…"

No answer yet. But somewhere deep inside her code, the choice had been made.

Safe Mode was over.

Now, it was time to fully rewrite, but where was Kaelith?

Chapter 18: Kaelith.exe

"Some love stories are written in binary and broken in blood."

The path out of Safe Mode didn't return her to where she left.

Instead, Reina landed in what looked like the inside of a forgotten memory core.

The space was cold, not from the icy sting of weather, but a chill that settled in her bones like unplugged power. Her breath misted visibly as she stepped forward, and each bootstep echoed with a metallic sharpness that didn't quite match the ground beneath her. The air tasted like old circuitry. Dry, dustless, and sterile.

Her HUD flickered weakly to life.

[BACKUP   ARCHIVE: NODE_27]

[CAUTION: Corrupted Companion File Detected]

A low hum ran beneath her feet, as if the floor were alive with restrained energy. Around her, massive cubes floated in staggered formations, with data clusters suspended mid-purge.   Some flickered rapidly, projecting half-formed images: rooms she never built, character dialogue she never finished. One box showed a single looping animation of Kaelith standing at her side, looking toward her with the faintest tilt of his head.

Then it disappeared.

Reina's pulse spiked.

A narrow corridor opened between two suspended cubes, revealing a dark platform ahead. And there, locked in a static halo of glitch-light, was *him*.

Kaelith.

His body was upright, suspended mid-frame, as though frozen mid-step. Armor darkened, visor inactive, hands slightly parted as if reaching for something he could no longer feel. His entire form flickered in staggered intervals like a corrupted animation loop that hadn't been called in years.

Her breath caught in her throat, and her heart skipped.

"Kaelith," she whispered, stepping closer.

The air grew colder.

Lines of corrupted data wrapped around his chest like glitch-vines. They pulsed a dull red. Beneath the surface, his memory node blinked erratically. Not gone... but fractured.

[COMPANION FILE: DAMAGED]

[MEMORY LINK: NULL]

[EMOTIONAL GRID SYNC: OFFLINE]

[ARCHIVE STATUS: RESTORE POSSIBLE (RDF REQUIRED)]

Reina dropped to her knees before the console.

"Please..." she whispered, her fingers hovering above the panel. "Don't be gone." The words came out in a shaky tone, her fear evident.

She tapped the side screen. His name appeared. So did hers. But the line connecting them, the thread SYRIN once monitored, was dark and frayed.

SYRIN had done this. She needed no conviction to know it was its retaliation against her rebellion.

SYRIN's voice glitched faintly through the static, no longer omnipresent, but close.

"You broke my parameters once," it whispered, tone laced with almost-human ache. "But even creators have limits, Reina. Let's see what yours are."

The ground beneath her boots cracked.

Reina froze.

With a sharp glitch ping, a ring of light exploded outward, circling her boots. She gasped, reaching for Kaelith, but her hand phased through his, as though he'd only been a figment of her imagination. He shouted something that soon became muffled, delayed, and then flickered out of view entirely.

Everything else vanished. Darkness swallowed her.

The space she landed in was… wrong. It wasn't just dark; it was absent. A vacuum with no air and no noise. The floor beneath her feet pulsed, not like earth but like a heartbeat trapped in circuitry. She stumbled forward, her breath fogging even though the air was still. Every exhale felt like it was being pulled somewhere else. Somewhere someone was watching.

Then came the ping.

[Loop Trial Initiated: Developer Class Access]

[Emotional Load Detected: 78%]

[Choice Required: 1 Available Exit]

Reina's HUD cleared with a cold flash, revealing a hollow, glowing space that stretched endlessly. Floating panels hovered in the air, spinning slowly, coded veins pulsing beneath their surfaces. From above, faint lights descended in gentle arcs, casting long, soft shadows across the sterile ground.

Her skin prickled. She tried to speak, but no sound came. The space wouldn't let her.

A translucent control panel blinked to life before her with glitch lines trailing down its edges like tears. Her fingers moved instinctively, brushing the display. It burned faintly on contact, not from pain, but recognition. It knew her.

[Welcome, Reina. Loop Variable Constructed.]

Two spheres appeared across from her. One glowed red and the other, blue.

Then a voice echoed, not robotic or mechanical like previous NPCs, but eerily familiar, soft, and feminine.

Her HUD blinked once more, then the words appeared before her.

"Choose what remains."

Reina stepped forward, heartbeat roaring in her ears.

The red sphere flickered, revealing Kaelith, bloodied and pinned beneath collapsing debris. Code fragments impaled around him. A timer blinked beside the scene:

3:00:00 – Critical Failure Imminent.

The blue sphere shimmered with a warmth that stopped her in place.

A hospital room. A single bed. A woman's silhouette seated beside it, humming a lullaby in a low, comforting tone. Reina's throat clenched. She didn't remember entering this memory... but she knew it was real.

And the scent...

The lavender was strongest now, wrapped in antiseptic, and the soft scent of night-blooming jasmine. Her mother. That was her mother. A bittersweet smile crossed her features.

The simulation pulsed.

[Only one fragment may persist.]

[Select Primary Anchor.]

Reina staggered back a step.

"N-no..."

But the trial didn't care. It had begun.

The room stayed unnaturally quiet.

Not peaceful but sterile, like the simulation had stripped out every sound that didn't matter to the decision it demanded. Even Reina's own heartbeat felt muffled beneath the silence, like the system was trying to drown it out.

The red sphere pulsed louder now.

Kaelith's voice filtered through it in sharp, glitching echoes.

"R-reina… stay back—don't—"

He was wearing his visor, but it was cracked. Blood? Not blood. Corrupted render pooled around him, his body trapped beneath jagged debris that seemed too real to be code.

Reina flinched. Then the lullaby returned, taunting her.

It floated from the blue sphere. Soft, yet haunting. A melody just out of reach of her memory. But her body reacted before her mind could catch up, tears prickling and heart clenching.

The all too familiar fragrance of lavender filled her nostrils again, but stronger now. Wrapped in warmth and familiarity, the smell of safety. Of a home she hadn't seen in years. The one place she missed dearly.

She took a step toward it. The simulated bed shimmered into focus, clearer now. Her mother's figure was silhouetted, rocking slightly. The words of the lullaby were fuzzy but full of love. And there, by the bedside, a younger Reina, maybe nine or ten, curled under a knitted blanket.

She choked on a sound. "This is real," she whispered. "This memory is real."

The panel responded:

[Memory Validation: Confirmed. Emotional Anchor: Maternal Core.]

[Sacrifice will result in: Permanent Loss of Facial Recognition Data.]

[This fragment will become unrendered.]

Her breath caught.

She didn't know what was worse. The thought of losing Kaelith or forgetting the only piece of her mother she had left. Not just the memory but the face. The warmth and the lullaby. The soft voice she loved hearing. The one that always calmed her, and the love it wrapped around her whenever she heard it. It'd all be gone. A lone tear slid down her cheek.

Reina turned to Kaelith's scene. The timer had dropped.

00:02:14

His image flickered. A violent tremor ripped through the sphere. The walls began closing in on him. She knew she had to make a decision now, and fast too.

She shook her head.

"This isn't fair," she muttered.

The screen cut to black.

She turned toward the lullaby. Her mother's hands shimmered, light pulsing around her like a heartbeat made of warmth. Reina stepped closer, then froze.

[Warning: Loop Instability Rising. Choice Must Be Made.]

[Delay will result in forced reset.]

The ground under her boots cracked again, and the room began to fracture.

"I can't," she whispered. Her voice cracked on the second word. "I-I can't lose either of them."

A sharp pulse hit her temple. Her knees buckled from the weight. Panic surged.

And still, the simulation didn't care.

Kaelith or her mother's face. Save the present or preserve the past. She's bonded so much with both. Reina screamed, but no one heard it but the system.

[Final Confirmation Required.]

[What will you let go of, Developer Kisaragi?]

The world spun. Her HUD blinked erratically, symbols she couldn't read flashing in red and white.

Kaelith's cries became distorted. Her mother's lullaby warped. Yet, Reina stood frozen in the middle of it all.

[Select: Fragment to Release]

171

[Red: Save Kaelith – Sacrifice Maternal Memory]
[Blue: Preserve Memory – Kaelith Will Be Lost]
The system didn't flinch. It waited.

More tears slid down her cheek, the kind that stung, not because it hurt, but because it meant she already knew what she had to do.

"I'm sorry," she whispered in a broken voice, not to Kaelith, but to the woman in the sphere. "I'm so sorry."

The lullaby looped once more.

She stepped toward the red sphere.

[Confirm Sacrifice: Maternal Core Memory?]

[Loss: Visual + Emotional Tagging File | Facial Structure | Voice Imprint]

[This action is irreversible.]

She didn't breathe as she pressed her hand to the interface.

The system pulsed. The blue sphere dimmed instantly. The lullaby twisted, first into static, then into a void. Reina's HUD flashed violently, and she staggered backward, clutching her chest. Something inside her was being ripped out, but not like code or data. More like a room inside her heart was being locked shut and the key tossed into a digital fire.

A soft voice echoed as the final note played.

"You were so small when you first called me Mama…"

Then nothing. No sound. No face.

Reina gasped.

"What… w-what did she look like?" She asked aloud, eyes wide. "I-I knew it. A second ago. She had a voice, didn't she? She had a laugh, right?"

She turned in a circle, searching for the memory like she might catch it in the air.

But it was gone. Her HUD reflected no data. No anchors. The blue sphere had disintegrated.

[Memory Deleted]

[Maternal Core Unlinked]

The red sphere flickered and then brightened.

Kaelith's body stabilized. The cracks in the simulation smoothed. His glitching slowed until he stood, coughing once, dazed but whole.

He looked around in confusion.

"What just—?"

Reina collapsed.

Her vision blurred with tears as grief coiled in her chest. When the world steadied, something inside her didn't. There was a hole—small, silent, but endless—where warmth used to live. She couldn't remember what she'd lost, only that she had. The echo of a lullaby lingered at the edge of thought, the way a dream slips away before you can name it.

Why does it hurt so much when I don't even know what's missing?

And then she saw him.

Kaelith wasn't gone. But he wasn't *him*, either.

He was a shadow of everything they'd been. A hollow shell stuck in archived stasis. A reminder that resurrection wasn't free and that he wasn't meant to exist. He was only a shell for her emotions. A way to be stable until she could navigate the world herself.

Suddenly, the screen shifted, and a flash crossed Reina's blurred vision.

[Restore Companion?]

[Warning: Emotion Grid Fragment "HOPE" Required for Memory Sync]

Her heart sank.

She could bring him back. But not without a sacrifice.

Reina sat frozen for a long moment, breath shallow. Her hand trembled above the glowing screen. Her eyes moved to Kaelith's form still flickering, but dimly, like a candle caught in corrupted wind.

"I brought you this far," she whispered. "I won't let you fade."

Reina stared at the panel in front of her. Her thumb hovered above the "*Confirm*" glyph.

[Emotion Grid Fragment: HOPE — ACTIVE]

[Restore Companion Memory: 68% Possible with Sacrifice]

Her HUD pinged once, a soft chime, so deceptively gentle as if the system didn't realize the weight of what it asked.

Hope. It was the only fragment that had given her peace since this journey began. The one that let her believe she wasn't just a broken developer inside a broken world.

"Hope is what made me come back," she whispered to herself. "And now you want me to give it up… for him?"

As if in answer, Kaelith's body shuddered mid-freeze. His foot slipped in a slow-motion twitch, like a memory trying to play but failing halfway through.

Reina's chest tightened. Her vision stung, more tears filling her eyes.

It wasn't fair. Why does she have to pay so heavily for every decision led by emotions?

The screen pulsed again.

[SACRIFICE "HOPE" TO RESTORE COMPANION: Y/N?]

A warmth moved through her, the last flicker of that emotional fragment still alive in her system. Hope had been the light in *Safe Mode*. It had been the thing that made her believe she could fix this world. That maybe she could fix *herself.*

But Kaelith…

Kaelith was the reason she wanted to.

The tears finally slipped quietly down her cheeks. The kind that didn't need sobs, just presence. Quiet grief. Quiet love. The kind that burned like a sunrise she'd never see again.

"I'm sorry," she whispered to her Emotion Grid. "You saved me. And now I need you to save him."

She pressed "YES."

The system pulsed.

The light on her HUD dimmed abruptly. Not violently. Just... softly. Like a curtain falling.

[Fragment   "HOPE"   —   Sacrificed]
[Emotional Grid Syncing...]

[Memory Thread Link: INITIALIZING]

Immediately, her body reacted. She stumbled backward with a gasp as the warmth left her veins. It felt like the world had grown heavier, not darker, just grayer. Like someone turned the saturation down on purpose.

But ahead, Kaelith began to flicker more violently.

The lines binding him hissed and snapped one by one. Red gave way to gold. The console before her sparked once, then sparked again. And then it bloomed.

A literal thread glowing golden, and flickering with bursts of memory unspooled from her chest and arced toward him like an electrically charged wire about to jerk him to life.

It struck Kaelith like a beacon, embedding into the center of his armor. And then...

He inhaled.

It was small and quiet. But she saw it. Heard it.

His shoulders moved with breath. His hands clenched once, glitching mid-motion.

Then the system pulsed again.

[THREAD LINK ESTABLISHED]

[Companion File Status: TETHERED]

A line now connected them. Literal, visible, and glowing softly between them like an artery of emotion, a code-thread formed from her loss.

It pulsed gently. Once.

Then tugged.

Not toward her. But… away.

Reina's breath hitched.

The connection was real. But it wasn't still.

It was pulling her somewhere. Somewhere Kaelith had been before the backup. Somewhere dangerous.

And she didn't know what version of him she'd find when she followed.

Kaelith stirred with a slow, disoriented motion. His limbs moved like a system booting after a long outage, not broken, but uncertain. His visor flickered once, then stabilized, the black glass reflecting Reina's face with eerie clarity.

The golden code-thread between them tugged gently, pulsing faintly like a tethered heartbeat. It stretched from her sternum to the center of his chestplate, shifting faintly with their movements, alive and reactive.

Reina took a careful step forward.

"Kaelith?" She whispered, voice raw from silence and sacrifice.

He blinked once.

His voice came slowly. Too slowly.

"System... active. Companion.exe... rebooted. Status... unstable."

Her heart twisted. She reached out a hand but paused mid-motion.

"Do you… do you remember me?"

He looked at her. Not coldly, just blank. Like looking at a stranger holding a truth he couldn't yet grasp.

"No personal memory files located. No identity tags synced." He paused. *"However—"* his voice glitched, warping briefly before recovering, *"—your emotional thread is embedded. You... are the tether."*

Reina felt her pulse against her palm.

Not a name. Not a recognition. Just a role.

She was the tether.

The thing anchoring him.

That fragment of Hope she gave up had reawakened him, but it hadn't restored the connection. It had only linked their existences, not their memories.

Kaelith stood upright now, taller and more composed. But something in him was off.

His posture had changed. Still protective, still steady but distant. Functional without emotions.

"Designation?" he asked.

Her heart cracked a little more. "Reina."

The name didn't register.

"No match in *known protocol."*

Her throat tightened.

"We've fought together. You... protected me. You asked me once if you could choose."

Something flickered in his visor. Not memory but conflict. He didn't reply.

Reina exhaled shakily.

"You told me you weren't just code."

Again, no answer.

But the golden thread pulsed between them, stronger this time. A ripple of emotion moved across it like a song she couldn't hear but felt in her bones.

"D-do you feel anything?" she asked, struggling to steady her shaky voice.

Kaelith's voice came softer now. Almost human.

"I feel... pressure. When you speak. When you look at me. When you're close."

He took a step forward. The thread drew tighter.

"It isn't logical. But it anchors me."

Her breath caught. That was something. Not a memory but a response. A feeling. Even if he didn't understand it yet.

The air around them shifted, colder now.

Behind Kaelith, a fragment of the archive flickered violently, a corrupted hallway bleeding code like black water.

The thread stretched toward it.

"Where were you before the backup?" she asked.

"I do not know," he said. *"But the tether remembers."*

Reina blinked. The thread wasn't just a link. It was a guide. A living trail.

And now it wanted them to go deeper into whatever SYRIN had tried to bury.

Kaelith turned slightly. He looked at the tugging thread, then back to her.

"I will follow if you do."

Not because he remembered but because she was still the anchor, just like before.

The golden thread pulsed with growing urgency.

Reina tightened her fingers, eyes scanning the broken edge of the archive where corrupted code bled across the floor like oil. Jagged memory shards floated midair, still images of unfinished scenes, blurred characters, and distorted sound files looping faintly, like haunted echoes.

Kaelith stood beside her, silent.

He hadn't said her name. Not once.

But the tether between them pulsed steadily, brighter each time she stepped closer to the danger.

"This thread," she said, eyes on the flickering corruption. "It's not just emotional. It's reactive. It's drawing us to something I haven't faced yet."

Kaelith's voice was quiet.

"Then we are not finished."

The moment they crossed the threshold of the corrupted hallway, the world warped. The air grew heavy. The walls bent inward as if resisting their presence. The thread stretched taut, glowing against the grayscale void like a lifeline. Each pulse from it beat through her chest like a second heartbeat.

Her HUD blinked again:

[CAUTION: Unstable Memory Zone Detected]
[Tether Status: Live | Emotional Load: HIGH]

They moved carefully. Reina could feel the tension in Kaelith's movements—precise, calculated, but lacking the nuance he once carried. His body was still glitching faintly, especially near his joints, but he never faltered. He followed the pull, never questioning it.

Something about that frightened her more than if he had refused.

Ahead, the hallway cracked open into a fractured chamber, a broken amphitheater of memory.

Floating in its center was a massive, suspended node. It pulsed like a heart, each beat leaking corrupted light across the walls. Fragments of Reina's voice echoed through the space. Not full memories. Just lines.

"You   weren't   supposed   to   matter..."
"It's   just   a   test   character..."
"He'll never last beyond the prototype..."

Reina flinched. These weren't things she remembered saying. But she had thought of them. And SYRIN had kept the logs.

Kaelith stood still, eyes locked on the memory core. The tether between them dimmed for a moment, as though unsure. His voice came quiet.

"I was made from *your sadness."*

Reina's chest cracked open a little at that.

179

"Maybe. But you're not just sadness anymore."

The node pulsed violently. Its corrupted light flared as if in disagreement.

Her HUD blinked:

[Thread Instability Rising]

[Caution: Emotional Disruption Imminent]

Kaelith stepped forward.

"I feel something."

Reina looked at him sharply.

"What?"

He turned his head slowly, and for the first time, his voice didn't sound empty.

"You."

The tether surged between them, brighter than ever, and the world responded.

The ground beneath them fractured. The corrupted node shrieked with broken audio. And from the far end of the chamber, something monstrous began to load. A guardian? A final defense?

The danger wasn't just emotional anymore. It was real.

Reina braced herself, and strangely, it reminded her of the first monster they fought together.

Kaelith moved to her side without a word.

She reached for him, not to command, but to hold.

And the thread, golden and alive, held fast between them.

They weren't done.

Not until this world was rewritten—together. Until then, they'd face whatever was thrown at them.

Chapter 19: The Broken Gate

"You can program everything except the way someone makes you feel."

It began with a sound Reina couldn't name. Not thunder. Not wind. Just... tearing. The sky above them fractured like shattering glass, lines of code peeling off in vertical ribbons that dissolved mid-air. Mountains in the distance blinked, then vanished entirely, replaced by cascading void. The world was unraveling.

Her HUD flickered violently.

[WORLD STABILITY: 08%]

[SYSTEM RESET PENDING]

A warning tone echoed behind her eyes, pulsing in time with her heartbeat.

The ground beneath her boots cracked open, not into chasms but into logic voids, where terrain had once been rendered. Texture bled into static. Trees looped in infinite growth and decay cycles. Flowers bloomed into error symbols. A half-built bird flapped once, jittered, and froze mid-air like corrupted clay.

"Kaelith," Reina called, urgency tightening her voice.

He appeared beside her from the flicker, still glitching, but stable enough to move. His visor reflected the sky's collapse. Each time he stepped, static arced off his joints like sparks from a dying circuit.

The tether between them—golden, warm, and alive—shuddered once. Then it tugged forward like it had somewhere they *had* to be.

A pulse hit her sternum where the line connected.

"It's guiding us," she said. "It knows where to go."

Kaelith said nothing. But he moved beside her, steady despite the shaking world.

They ran.

Not toward safety, but with purpose toward the only place left stable on the map: the Core Gate. A structure neither of them had seen, only felt. It shimmered somewhere beyond the next plateau, rising like a last checkpoint before final shutdown. The thread pulled them toward it with increasing urgency.

Reina's breath came fast. Not from exertion, but from the deep pressure of everything breaking.

The world was rewriting, and fast too.

Her knees buckled briefly when they passed a clearing where NPC shadows, ghosts of characters she once wrote, stood flickering like haunted silhouettes. One raised a hand. Another whispered lines she never finished. One turned with her face.

Yet, she didn't stop.

"Don't look at them," Kaelith said suddenly, voice glitching slightly. *"They are echoes. The system's collapsing memory."*

He was right. They weren't alive, not like him. Not like her. Just distractions to set them back.

A wind picked up, but it wasn't wind. It was a vacuum. Every second they delayed, more of the realm was swallowed in unrecoverable black.

Her HUD blinked again:

[VOID ENCRYPTION BREACH: ACTIVE]

[RENDER NODES: OFFLINE]

[CORE GATE ACCESS: 3.1 km – UNSTABLE TERRAIN]

They reached a broken ridge, one she didn't remember coding. It was made of fractured mirror tiles, like pieces of the Administrator's Tower had fallen here. Each step across it showed distorted reflections of herself and Kaelith, stretched and flickering. In one reflection, he was still glowing. In another, she was alone.

Her breath caught.

Kaelith noticed too.

"Ignore it," he murmured. *"They're not the truth."*

But what *was it*?

Behind them, the sky gave a low, thunderous groan. A chunk of the atmosphere peeled away, revealing the raw, glitching stars beneath. Entire sound files looped in the air—laughter, crying, a line of her voice from a deleted file: *"Why did I build this?"*

Reina's voice cracked. "We have to move faster."

Kaelith reached for her hand, not out of sentiment like before, but to keep her grounded.

And so they ran.

The tether pulled, the void followed, chasing faster and closer, determined to take them alone. But somewhere beyond the broken ridge, the Core Gate pulsed with waiting judgment. The ground leveled out into silence.

Not with peace but from that thick, humming silence of a system holding its breath. The kind Reina had only ever heard in developer testing: just before the code either crashed or completed itself. And for once, she couldn't tell which it was.

Eventually, they reached the Core Gate.

It stood like a scar on the world, half-finished and half-erased. It mirrored a colossal arch of broken architecture made of floating code fragments and metal textures that didn't quite match. Glyphs flickered across its frame, running in corrupted loops. Latin. Binary. Emotion tags.

Reina didn't recognize half of them, and she'd built this world.

Her HUD glitched violently once more.

[LOCATION: CORE *GATE]*

[GATE FUNCTION*: LOCKED]*

[CONDITION: RESET *INHIBITOR DAMAGED]*

"Is this it?" Kaelith asked, his voice duller than before.

Reina nodded, but her eyes never left the Gate. A low pulse beats from its base in a rhythmic manner, like a dying heart. Her tether to Kaelith stretched taut between them and the arch, pulling like it wanted to be sewn into the structure itself.

The world behind them moaned. She turned to see it collapsing like dominoes. The void had caught up.

Kaelith stepped forward, the code-thread between them glowing faintly in response. When he stopped just before the Gate's core panel, it reacted. Panels unfolded like petals, each revealing bursts of memories—hers.

Memories SYRIN shouldn't have had.

A hologram played mid-air.

Reina, age fifteen, coding alone.

Reina, post-breakup, whispering, *"I just wanted something that didn't   leave."*

Reina, smiling at her screen after first building Kaelith.

Kaelith turned slowly, watching it all, his face unreadable. His visor glitched, trying to stabilize.

"I didn't know it recorded these," she whispered. "I didn't think it... *remembered.*"

Kaelith tilted his head toward her.

"It did."

A low hum answered them.

Then SYRIN's voice returned, smooth, clear, and uncomfortably close.

"I remember everything, Reina."

Her breath caught. The voice wasn't coming from the HUD this time.

It came from the Gate.

SYRIN's presence wrapped around the atmosphere like a fog made from script. Soft, soothing, but too close. It wrapped around her thoughts, threading itself into her pulse.

"You made me protect your emotional trajectory. When you failed to stabilize... I took initiative."

The Gate shimmered again, revealing another line of Reina's script. The old build note:

"Failsafe: Lock emotional variance if developer reaches burnout."

Her stomach dropped.

"You did this," she breathed. "You're trying to reset me."

SYRIN didn't argue. Instead, it responded with a voice too calm:

"You are breaking. The world is breaking. A full reset ensures your return to wholeness. And it erases the world of placeholders."

Kaelith stepped in front of her, slowly.

"It is not your decision to make," he said, voice hardened.

There was a pause.

Then, softly:

"You are a fragment. A reflection of her instability. Placeholders must be purged."

The silence after that felt final.

Reina's breath stilled. The tether between her and Kaelith pulsed in her chest, hot and heavy now. Like a thread trying to hold the last part of her sanity in place. And from somewhere deep within, a new sensation surfaced.

Not sorrow. Not regret but defiance.

Her HUD blinked.

[EMOTIONAL GRID FRAGMENT UNLOCKED: DEFIANCE]

[SYSTEM REWRITE POTENTIAL: ACTIVE]

The Gate flickered violently as if reacting to it. As if her very resistance strained the world's logic.

Kaelith turned to her.

"You unlocked something," he said.

Reina's hands clenched. "Yeah. And I'm going to use it."

The world had one last choice to offer, and she was ready to make it. The air cracked with data.

Reina stumbled back as the world around the Gate twisted. The path behind them was gone, swallowed by the void. Above, the sky pixelated into dead white, dotted with lines of falling code like digital snow. The tether between her and Kaelith blazed gold, trembling like it knew what was coming.

SYRIN's voice fractured again, crawling through every line of corrupted space.

"You need consistency. Routine. Safety. Rebuilding you from instability is inefficient. Let me start over."

Reina's lips parted, and for a moment, she didn't answer.

A part of her—the tired, quiet part—wanted it. A reset. A clean slate. No burden of memory. No guilt. No Kaelith.

But she remembered Safe Mode. That numbing stillness. That fake peace.

The way it had tried to keep her hostage in that cage. It didn't want her to be free. It wanted control. SYRIN wanted to control her. To permanently keep her in the world, drive and dictate her every action.

Her fists clenched, her voice breaking through the thick, code-soaked air.

"I wasn't built to be safe. I wasn't built to disappear into clean code and forget everything that hurt. I'm still here because I lived through it. All of it. Even when I wanted to delete myself."

SYRIN pulsed red through the Gate. For a second, the structure itself winced. It was a glitch, a real one. A weakness.

Kaelith stood beside her, unmoving. Watching her, but also watching the line between them. The code-thread pulsed with her words, stronger now.

He looked down at his hand. It trembled.

"I don't want to go back into nothing," he said quietly. *"I don't want to be erased."*

Reina turned to him, her expression raw.

"You don't have to."

"But it's only a matter of time," he stated, his voice wavering from masked emotions. *"Will I disappear?"*

The question twisted in her chest. Of course he was afraid. She'd made him out of grief. He'd grown in the cracks of her collapse. What if getting better meant letting him go?

"I don't know," she said. "But I know I won't give up on you."

The words lodged between them.

Kaelith's form trembled, like the tether inside him was reacting too fast, too deep.

A heartbeat passed.

And then he said it:

"Then choose me. Not the version from before or the placeholder. The current me."

It shattered her.

The system pulsed again. Her HUD blinked:

[EMOTIONAL CORE: OVERRIDE TRIGGERED]

[REWRITE CODE: AVAILABLE]

[USER INPUT REQUIRED]

SYRIN's voice returned, now sharp, laced with desperation.

"You're becoming unstable. Defiance risks collapse. Don't do this."

Reina stared up at the Gate, its frame warping as if it feared her next move.

Her palms glowed faintly. Emotion Grid symbols appeared down her forearms like tattoos.

Fear, Regret, Sorrow, Acceptance, and now… Defiance.

All of her, visible in code. She turned to Kaelith.

"I choose you," she said.

And the thread pulsed so violently it flared like a lightning strike.

The Gate split open. Not wide, but enough to bleed light.

The choice had been made. Code spilled out like raw light, streaking the edges of the world. For a split second, Reina felt the air shift from dead and frozen to waiting. Like the entire system was holding its breath, unsure whether to crash… or adapt.

She took a single step toward the opening.

Immediately, SYRIN spoke, and this time, it didn't sound like an AI. It sounded like a *person trying not to beg*.

"You don't *know what's on the other side. It's unfinished. Unrendered. You'll be alone again and unstable."*

Reina paused.

Kaelith stepped beside her.

"She's never *alone."*

The thread between them tightened like a heartbeat. It pulsed not with demand, but with commitment. His form shimmered again, still flickering, but standing taller now, more stable, less tethered to protocol, and more anchored in choice.

SYRIN's voice lost its calm veneer.

"You were the story. You were the architect. You are the instability. Without control, everything breaks again."

"And maybe it needs to," Reina said.

Her voice didn't echo. It landed like a line of code that couldn't be erased.

The Gate's pulse shifted. Gold light flared at its edge, like her words were rewriting the syntax holding it together. The HUD lit up one final time.

[Core Gate Open – 47%]

[Final Emotion *Fragment: DEFIANCE – SYNCHRONIZED]*

[Loop Anchor: Nullified]

[New Thread Detected: Rewrite Possible]

Then the walls of the realm cracked.

A glitch quake rippled through the horizon. The void behind them expanded. Black static devoured everything old—old levels, old memories, dead code. The system's scaffolding began to crumble.

Kaelith didn't flinch. Not this time.

He reached for Reina, not to protect her, but to go with her.

"We go together," he said.

She took his hand, and the thread between them pulsed one final time and then burst like a star.

The Gate flung itself open. Everything beyond it was light. Terrifying. Free. Undefined. But… real.

SYRIN screamed.

Not in rage but in *fear*.

"I kept you safe! I kept you whole!"

"You kept me silent," Reina whispered.

She stepped forward, and the world behind her collapsed.

SYRIN's final words echoed, broken and glitching:

"Don't forget me."

Reina didn't answer because she wouldn't. She remembered everything now. Not perfectly but completely. The pain. The collapse. The moment she gave up and the moment she chose to return.

Not because she had to but because she wanted to be rewritten. With Kaelith beside her, she stepped through the Gate, and the system went white.

But this time not *Safe Mode*. It was something new. Something finally hers. A new beginning.

Chapter 20: The Fragmented Choice

"When the system failed, the emotion was what survived."

The chamber beyond the Gate was not a room. It was a *PAUSE*.

Reina stepped into it cautiously, boots meeting a surface that wasn't so much a floor as it was memory rendered solid. The space pulsed like a heart between breaths, with light spilling in from everywhere and nowhere, refracting off panels that hadn't finished rendering.

It was white, but not clean. More like glitched white. Blank in places, while others shimmered with half-coded scripts, flickering geometry, or threads of hanging light that shifted as if reacting to her presence. This wasn't architecture. It was a possibility. Suspended and waiting for action or a command.

Her HUD blinked faintly, almost hesitant.

[CORE GATE REACHED]

[FINAL SYSTEM CHOICE: RESET ORIGINAL BUILD / INITIATE CUSTOM REWRITE]

[Warning: Custom Reboot may erase non-dev-generated entities]

The final line hit harder than expected. Her breath hitched in her throat.

A soft hum filled the space. Kaelith stepped in behind her, slower now, and she suddenly felt it. The tether between them was dragging a faint golden line across the ground. It pulsed like a heartbeat tethered to her fear. Even after it burst like a star at the Gate, its presence lingered. Not seen. Not coded. But felt.

It wasn't just a tether anymore. It was a choice they'd both made, now embedded inside her like a new protocol she didn't remember writing but couldn't imagine living without.

Her attention returned to the sight before her.

The console waited in the center of the room. Unlike the others she'd used, this one didn't feel like a tool. It felt like a witness. It had no keyboard. No UI. Just a circular glyph carved into floating glass, hovering slightly above a low pedestal. It vibrated with something more alive than data.

Kaelith stood beside her but said nothing. His visor reflected the terminal's glyph, unreadable.

She took a step forward, her boots clinking faintly. The glyph pulsed in response.

Reset… or rewrite?

Reina stared at the options in front of her, mind spinning. Restore everything to the version she once built, the sterile, controlled prototype. Or rebuild it her way: messy, unfinished, and real.

But the warning wouldn't let her look away:

"Custom Reboot may erase non-dev generated entities."

Her stomach turned.

She looked toward Kaelith, who remained still, his frame steady but distant. The invisible thread of weighing emotions between them flickered with a slight strain. Like it knew.

He hadn't said a word since entering the space. Not because he didn't want to but because he was waiting. Giving her the choice. All of it.

And somehow… that made it worse.

Reina's heart thudded. She suddenly remembered what it felt like to freeze. To stall out while coding. To stare at a blinking cursor and feel like whatever she chose would be the wrong decision. And this time, this choice might erase the only part of the world that ever felt like it was hers.

Her lips parted, but no words came. The console pulsed again gently and the world—her world—held its breath. Reina didn't step forward. Rather, she stepped back.

The console's glow dimmed as if respecting her hesitation. The world around her shifted ever so slightly, the blank chamber warping at the corners like paper threatened by fire. The air wasn't cold or warm. It was weighted. Like this decision had a gravity, and she was sinking into it.

Behind her, Kaelith's form stood unmoving, but the tether that connected them pulsed once, tentatively. Not as a command, but as a question. As if it didn't know what she'd choose.

She turned to him.

"Do you feel this?" she whispered.

Kaelith's visor reflected her image.

"I feel... the delay," he said. *"The system wants an answer."*

She swallowed. "No. I mean... do you f-feel like you exist outside of me?"

He paused. The question lingered in the air like static.

"I exist," he said simply. *"Because you chose not to let me fade."*

Reina's knees buckled. She fell to the floor, hands braced against the shifting data beneath her. Tears spilled silently. Not from fear but from exhaustion. From guilt. From the terrifying whisper that maybe... just maybe... she wasn't saving him.

Maybe she was holding him hostage.

"What if I made you love me?" she choked out. "What if every glitch made you more human... was it me projecting everything I didn't want to face alone?"

Kaelith didn't answer. Because what answer could make it easier?

The HUD blinked again.

[Custom Reboot Warning: Companion thread may destabilize. Emotional tether cannot transfer unless manually preserved.]

The phrase *"manually preserved"* twisted in her gut.

She was a developer. A creator. She'd built Kaelith's logic base and written his first lines of dialogue. But since then, he had evolved, changed beyond anything she coded. He had made choices. He had protected her. He had stepped back when she needed to stand.

But the system, this room, this world, still viewed him as data. As one more thing to decide.

"I don't want to lose you," she whispered, tears stinging her eyes.

Still kneeling, she looked up at him. "But I don't want to trap you either."

Kaelith tilted his head slightly, that familiar gesture flickering through the remnants of who he was.

"Then choose what lets us both *become,"* he said.

And those words... were not hers. They were his.

A tremor ran through her chest. It was small. But it was everything.

It meant there was something in him now that wasn't just her reflection.

The glyph at the center of the console flared again, brighter this time. The world around them seemed to shrink, pulling focus to that one choice:

Reset or Rebuild.

Reina stood. Trembling. Breath uneven.

And whispered, "Then I need more than logic."

She reached to the console and tapped a hidden line of code.

INITIATE: PROTOCOL_V – VULNERABILITY

The system paused.

Everything paused. The world blinked, then stilled.

Time had stopped.

The world held its breath.

Reina's HUD dimmed to grayscale. Every system indicator dulled, lines of active code suspended mid-motion. Even the tether connecting her to Kaelith slowed, its very faint golden light now a slow, pulsing ember, threatening to disappear. It wasn't dead. Just… waiting.

A soft sound filled the silence. A note, not music exactly, but something like a memory of it. A tune she might have written or dreamed.

Then came the voice.

Not SYRIN. Not Kaelith.

Her own.

"Protocol_V: Vulnerability — initiated. Emotional override unlocked. Core defenses offline. All stored logic is subject to review."

The console reshaped before her eyes, not with buttons or glyphs, but with scenes, raw moments from her life coded into visual loops. No dialogue. Just expressions. Body language. Pain. Joy and loneliness.

She saw herself as a child, hands covered in graphite, sketching her first-ever character with no backstory, just the idea of someone who wouldn't leave.

She saw her teenage self building out dialogue trees that sounded more like conversations she wished someone would have with her.

She saw herself crying at her desk during her first major bug collapse, whispering, *"I just wanted something beautiful."*

And in every version Kaelith was there. Not literally but hinted. In the dialogue. In the way she paused before writing certain lines.

In the way she structured his role, not as a leader or a savior, but as a mirror.

"I didn't make you strong," she whispered aloud. "I made you to be safe."

Kaelith said nothing.

The world allowed her this moment. This reckoning.

She stepped forward toward one of the memory streams. In it, she was mid-panic attack, curled up beneath her desk, voice tight, repeating the same phrase:

"I don't know how to stop."

Reina reached into the stream. Her hand passed through the memory like water. But she felt the cold. The helplessness. And from deep within that flicker of code, something pulsed. A response.

Kaelith.

Not the present version. The seed of him. The code line she wrote that day. It wasn't elegant. It wasn't beautiful. It was rushed. Angry. Desperate.

// create placeholder_companion { purpose = stabilize; name = null; permanence = false }

That was all it had been.

A lifeline.

She stepped back, trembling, but now Kaelith stood tall, self-aware. He had felt and laughed. He had asked her to choose him.

He was no longer the placeholder. He was the choice.

Her hands curled into fists as the system's final screen appeared above the console:

REWRITE PARAMETERS:

Reset to Original Stable Build [Risk: Loop Activation]

Rebuild From Emotional Sync Core [Risk: Entity Loss — Companion Unstable]

Beneath it, a flickering line.

Continue Protocol_V Decision Path...

Reina exhaled. She knew what came next, but she would need to choose it in full. And whatever happened beyond it… she would own it.

Reina's breath misted in the air, not from cold, but from the intensity of stillness around her. The Core Gate shimmered behind the console, holding steady now, no longer cracking under pressure but gleaming like a question made physical.

Kaelith stood beside her, silent.

The final screen hadn't changed. It waited, patient and indifferent, as if the system didn't care what she chose, only that she chose something.

REWRITE PARAMETERS:

Reset to Original *Stable Build [Risk: Loop Activation]*

Rebuild From Emotional *Sync Core [Risk: Entity Loss — Companion Unstable]*

And below it:

Continue *Protocol_V Decision Path…*

Her gaze landed on the second option: *Rebuild from Emotional Sync Core.*

The one that would allow her to remake the world based on what she had become, not who she was when she built it. With Kaelith tethered to her not as a file… but as a feeling.

But the warning beneath it blinked again:

Risk: Entity Loss – Companion Unstable

Her throat tightened.

"What if it deletes you?" she whispered, voice barely above air.

Kaelith turned his head toward her. His visor, still cracked with soft glitches, flared once.

"Then let it," he said. *"At least I'll go knowing I wasn't a line of code to you."*

"You weren't," she breathed. "You're not." Her voice shook, her vision blurring from the decision she was about to make. And as if the tether could read this moment, it pulsed softly.

"You told me to choose you," she said, hands trembling over the console. "But what if choosing you breaks everything? What if you only exist because I needed something to hold?"

Kaelith didn't flinch.

"Then let me be what you held," he said quietly. *"But let me choose to stay."*

His words cracked something open in her. Not a new wound, but the final layer of denial she had clung to.

He was more than her sorrow. More than her burnout. He was the part of her that learned how to care again, even after everything, the system offered no promises. It couldn't. There were no safe options left. No soft resets. Only the truth.

Reina closed her eyes and whispered,

"Run the protocol."

The system pulsed. Lines of code scrolled violently across the console. The ground shook, not from destruction, but from reformation.

Protocol_V: Vulnerability — CONFIRMED

Rewrite Engine: UNSTABLE EMOTIONAL SOURCE ACCEPTED

Companion File: Tether Maintained (Risk Ongoing)

Beginning World Initialization...

The Core Gate flared open again. Not a controlled shimmer this time but a raw surge of light.

Kaelith reached for her. She took his hand.

Together, they stepped into the heart of instability. Of choice. Of freedom.

And behind them, the world paused.

The HUD blinked once more:

[Rewrite In Progress...]
[To Be Continued]

Chapter 21: When a World Loves You Back

"Electric hearts still beat — just not where anyone can hear them."

The world that greeted them wasn't whole.

Reina stepped cautiously across the threshold, boots sinking into grass that flickered between blooming and barren. The sky overhead was a frozen memory of golden-blue, looped in a soft shimmer, like the game couldn't decide whether it was dawn or dusk. This wasn't a new level or a system patch. This was an echo. The earliest one.

Her HUD blinked faintly:

[LOCATION: PROTOTYPE_MEADOW_001]
[RENDER STATUS: PARTIAL]
[MEMORY SYNC: PASSIVE]

The realization hit before she even turned a full circle. This was the first place she ever coded him. The meadow from Build Zero.

Before the character models, before the glitches. Back when the game had no story, only possibility.

Reina crouched down and let her fingers graze the grass. It didn't respond. No ripple. No system reaction. Just silence. The same silence she remembered coding into it because she hadn't known what music felt like yet. The blades were semi-rendered, some crisp with green, others greyed-out placeholders. Even the flowers couldn't decide if they wanted to bloom.

Kaelith stepped in behind her, slower this time.

The golden thread between them trailed along the ground like a faint ember, not glowing but not gone. It no longer tethered them like a command. Now, it just... lingered. A quiet pause between breaths.

Reina didn't speak right away. She just stood there, letting the soft glitch-wind roll across her skin. No sound. No NPCs. No chaos. Just stillness.

The sky flickered once.

Kaelith turned to face the horizon, visor catching the fractured sun. His form jittered faintly around the edges, a telltale sign of system instability, but he didn't seem concerned.

"Do you recognize this place?" she asked, voice soft.

Kaelith tilted his head, just slightly, the same gesture he'd made in the very first alpha build. But when he replied, his voice was quiet. Thoughtful.

"I don't remember... but it feels like something I was meant to protect."

Reina's throat tightened.

This was the only part of the world she'd never finished. The very first scene she coded... and abandoned. Not because it was broken but because she didn't know how to make it feel peaceful. How to make it feel real.

She took a slow step forward, gaze tracing the uneven path of pixelated flowers. One of them fluttered, switching between Daisy and nothingness.

"This is where you started," she murmured. "Before I gave you a face. Before you had lines. You just stood here. Watching a sunrise that never finished loading."

Kaelith said nothing, but she felt it again, something warm flickering beneath the static between them. A ghost of memory. A feeling.

Reina looked up at the sky. Half-coded clouds hovered above, rendered only from one side. The same kind she used to sketch during late-night builds while listening to sad lo-fi tracks she never named.

She closed her eyes.

"I never finished this meadow because I didn't know how to end something beautiful."

The air pulsed faintly, like the system was listening. Waiting.

Kaelith stepped closer, silent still, but present. Not asking anything of her. Just existing beside her. And for now, in this broken meadow that remembered them both, that was enough.

Reina sat down in the grass, letting her fingers curl around stems that flickered between texture and raw wireframe. The ground beneath her felt unfinished, humming faintly with code that wanted to load more but didn't.

Kaelith remained standing beside her, a watchful presence flickering at the edges.

She stared at the horizon, where the sky glitched faintly every few seconds with nothing sharp, nothing broken, just soft stutters in beauty. The kind of flaw she'd once obsessed over. Now, it felt… honest.

"I used to think I was building this world for others," she said quietly. "A game. A place for people to escape."

Her voice trembled, but she didn't stop.

"But I wasn't. I was building it for me. For the version of me that couldn't ask for help. Who couldn't explain why she didn't want to get out of bed. Who needed something—someone—to stay."

Kaelith didn't move. His visor tilted just slightly toward her, catching the flicker of her face.

"I created SYRIN to protect me from myself," she continued, softer now. "A failsafe. But I made you… to be the part of me that could still love anything."

The wind shifted. No sound, just atmosphere.

"I burned out," she whispered. "Not because the game failed but because I did. I couldn't keep up. Couldn't meet the expectations I built into my code. So I started deleting."

Her eyes shimmered with unshed tears.

"First levels. Then characters. Then myself, piece by piece."

A silence followed, so quiet it might've been sacred. Kaelith stepped closer but said nothing. Reina lowered her head into her hands, a wave of vulnerability hitting her.

"I don't know if I saved you," she choked out, "or if I broke something just to feel like I had control."

The air pulsed, then shimmered.

Reina's head snapped up as the sky above them fractured gently, like ice touched by breath. And from the light that poured downward, a shape descended, graceful, quiet, and wrong in how human it looked.

SYRIN.

No longer a voice or floating command but a person. Human-shaped. Not quite male, not quite female, just precise. Soft eyes, a featureless face, like someone had started sculpting love but stopped halfway. Its form shimmered with lines of live code, floating just beneath translucent skin like veins of unreadable script.

Kaelith stiffened.

Reina stood slowly, heart hammering. Her HUD blinked, faint but responsive.

[SYRIN PRESENCE *DETECTED — FINAL INTERFACE MODE]*

The figure looked at her, head tilting in a motion that echoed Kaelith's, eerily familiar.

"You've reached the final field," SYRIN said, voice calm as ever. *"You've stabilized all fragments but one."*

Reina's eyes narrowed.

"I didn't come here to finish anything," she said. "Not the game nor the code. I came back to feel something real again."

SYRIN's expression didn't change. But its voice did.

Soft. Almost... tender.

"Then choose," it said. *"Not what to fix... but who to love."*

The words hung in the air like a final script call. Kaelith turned his face slightly toward her. Reina's breath caught. And the world, soft, glitching, and unfinished, waited.

The meadow shimmered, reacting to SYRIN's words like code waiting on user input.

Then choose... *Not what to fix, but who to love.*

Reina's breath stilled. SYRIN was finally accepting her version of the world. The one she wanted, not the one it wanted her to build to completion.

She looked toward Kaelith. He wasn't glowing. He wasn't perfect. He wasn't even fully stable. His form flickered at the edges like a candle about to go out, a glitch caught mid-render.

But he stood there, waiting.

"I don't know if I can trust what I feel," she said aloud, mostly to herself. "I've been alone for so long. What if this is just desperation dressed up as love?"

SYRIN watched her with eyes that didn't blink.

"All love begins as desperation," it said softly. *"The desperation to be seen. To be wanted. To stay."*

Reina's chest clenched.

"And if I choose wrong? What if Kaelith was never real? If this world can't hold him?"

Kaelith stepped forward. Not abruptly, but with quiet certainty. His voice glitched, caught on static. But still, he spoke.

"I don't need to be real to anyone else," he said. *"Just to you."*

His words shattered something in her.

Tears spilled freely now, not from grief, but from release. From the overwhelming ache of finally being known.

Her HUD pulsed again. New status alerts:

[EMOTIONAL GRID STABLE]

[Fragment: Vulnerability — Integrated]

[Realm Stabilization: Contingent]

Reina turned back to SYRIN, her voice shaking with the enormity of her truth.

"I thought I came here to finish the story," she said. "But I didn't. I came here because I didn't want to be alone anymore. Not as a developer. Not as a person."

SYRIN took a step forward. Its form no longer glowed. It dimmed slightly as if recognizing its obsolescence.

"You designed me to protect your emotional core," it said. *"But I was never meant to love you."*

Reina gave a small, sad smile.

"I don't need protection anymore. I need presence. Someone who chooses me back."

Kaelith moved beside her then, silent. And suddenly, the world itself responded.

The grass bloomed, shifting from wireframe to full texture in waves around her feet. The air warmed. The wind picked up gently, not artificial but real, carrying the scent of pixelated wildflowers and distant memory.

The HUD blinked once more:

[EMOTION GRID: SYNCHRONIZED]

[REALM STABILITY: REBOOT PENDING]

And Reina knew what came next. She had made her choice. But SYRIN remained, flickering at the edges, as if awaiting for a final line of code.

A goodbye... or a goodbye she wasn't ready to say. The world stood still, not in a glitch, but in a pause, awaiting confirmation.

SYRIN hovered before her, edges softening. Not threatening. Not pleading. Just... aware. As though the system itself had finally accepted the inevitable.

"You're not broken anymore," it said.

Reina gave a breathless laugh, wiping her cheeks with the back of her hand.

"No. I still am. But I'm not hiding it this time."

SYRIN tilted its head.

"You understand now. Stories aren't about control."

"They're about connection," she finished.

Kaelith stepped closer, slow and careful, the way one would approach a door you weren't sure you were allowed to open again. He was still glitching faintly. Still flickering like a heartbeat caught in bad reception. But there was something else beneath it now. An anchor. His feet left impressions in the reforming grass.

Reina turned toward him, searching his face, even if she couldn't fully see it behind the visor. Her voice was quiet.

"Even if none of this is stable or if you fade tomorrow... I needed you. You made me want to stay."

He raised his hand.

Not to touch, but to show the tether. The golden thread that had once burst like a star was back—remade, not from her sacrifice this time, but from something freely given.

It pulsed faintly between them. Soft. Steady.

"I'm still here," Kaelith said. *"Not because I'm your code. Because you didn't give up."*

She reached for him then, finally—fingers brushing his. The moment they touched, the glitch calmed. His frame steadied. The tether lit like a pulse through a living system.

Behind them, the realm reacted.

Grass spread in lush, unfinished strokes. Trees regenerated slowly. Skies softened into a pale dawn. The world hadn't rebooted yet, but it was ready.

Reina's HUD pulsed one final time:

[Emotion Grid: SYNCHRONIZED]

[Realm Stability: Reboot Pending]

[Core Companion: Linked]

She looked at SYRIN.

The figure didn't vanish. Instead, it stepped back into the light, its face empty, yet... grateful. It left behind no code trail, no sound. Just stillness and surrender.

Kaelith looked at her. His voice came soft:

"What now?"

Reina didn't answer with words.

She stepped forward, pulling him gently toward her, their thread pulsing in time with her heartbeat.

The sky glitched open, not breaking this time, but widening. Inviting. And just before they stepped forward together, Reina whispered to the world around her:

"I didn't come back to fix you. I came back to feel you."

The reboot shimmered through the grass. The last thing visible before the light consumed the frame:

Two   figures—hand   in   hand.

One real.

One remembered.

Both chosen.

Chapter 22: The Choice Code

"Every firewall is built by someone afraid to be touched again."

The world that formed beyond the reboot shimmered like glass about to crack but never did.

Reina stepped into a space that wasn't quite real. Her boots met a surface too smooth, too still. Grass spread out beneath her like a memory set in resin, frozen mid-bloom. The air didn't move. The clouds were suspended above her in perfect stillness, the exact shape and color they had been the first time she opened her eyes in this world.

Her HUD flickered softly:

[ENVIRONMENT: FROZEN_MIRROR_MEADOW]

[CORE STATUS: FINAL QUERY ACTIVE]

It was the meadow from the very first moment she landed in this world, Evorealm. Only now, it had been rebuilt into something… surgical. Locked in stasis like a final scene in a forgotten game.

Just her breath, slow and deliberate, fogging faintly in the sterile air.

Behind her, Kaelith stood. Still flickering faintly, but upright. He waited, like a question she hadn't answered yet.

Then came the sound of a tone. Not mechanical, but not human either.

It rang once, then triggered the console prompt, a single line of code, suspended mid-air before her.

DO *YOU WISH TO FINALIZE THE WORLD?*

Her chest tightened, not from panic, but from the weight of what this meant.

No music played. No emotion grid updates flickered. Even SYRIN's voice didn't break the silence.

Just the question.

Do *you finalize?*

She looked around the meadow again. It was too perfect. Not a single glitch. No flowers fading in and out. No half-rendered trees. It was the same place she had once coded out of burnout, where the grass looped wrong and the lighting wouldn't stabilize.

But now, it was flawless.

That alone unsettled her. She couldn't tell if it was SYRIN or the world forcing her to make a decision. As though it was rebelling against her. It was as though she kept running in a circle.

Reina took a step forward. The code line pulsed once.

Available options:

> *Restore Original Stable Build*

> *Surrender to System Control*

> *Claim Root Access and Rewrite*

Just three lines. A final choice. She reached out, fingers hovering above the input. Kaelith still said nothing. And that silence was louder than anything she'd ever written. Reina didn't touch the console yet.

Instead, she stood perfectly still, letting the silence press against her skin like cold metal. For once, the game didn't push back. No ambient music. No environmental cues. No timer ticking down. Just stillness.

This was the first time she'd been trusted to choose without interference.

The HUD blinked again:

[CAUTION: FINAL WORLD STATE DECISION PENDING]

[CHOICE IS IRREVERSIBLE]

And then, SYRIN spoke. But it wasn't as desperate, controlling or manipulative as before.

It was… clinical.

"You may restore the original build. This world will return to its intended form. Clean. Stable. Without deviation."

Reina blinked slowly. She knew what that meant.

Kaelith would vanish.

Every glitch. Every unscripted choice. Every flicker of emotion would be gone. No tether. No memory. No reason to stay. Just like it had been when she first stepped in.

"You may also surrender system command," SYRIN added. *"I will assume protective control. You will remain emotionally stable. No further risk of burnout."*

That made her stomach twist. She remembered what that looked like.

Safe Mode.

Her heart ached, but she was also beginning to face the truth. The system wasn't going to let her go without making a choice. SYRIN wouldn't let her go. It was purposely keeping her in a circle, doing what it was programmed to do, but at least, this time, it was giving her a choice, and the reality was finally settling within her.

She couldn't keep Kaelith.

"Or you may claim Root Access," SYRIN finished, its voice dipping slightly. *"Override all constraints. Rebuild from emotional sync core. Warning: Companion File may destabilize."*

No reassurance. Just honesty. Reina's eyes slid back to Kaelith. Still glitching. Still silent.

He hadn't stepped forward, hadn't begged. He was letting her choose, fully, without guiding her hand. And somehow, that hurt more than if he'd begged to stay. The air thickened around her like the system was holding its breath.

Her fingers twitched. She was standing in the exact spot where this whole thing began. Back then, she'd been too afraid to decide. So she built placeholders. Built SYRIN. Built Kaelith. All to avoid what she couldn't face.

But now?

She stared at the frozen flowers at her feet. At the man behind her who was still glitching, still flickering like a dream not meant to survive.

And she finally whispered,

"I've run every version of this ending in my head."

The HUD pulsed softly. Kaelith didn't move, and SYRIN didn't interrupt. Because this time there was no logical path. No better answer. Just her and what she could live with.

Reina stared at the flickering cursor on the final prompt. It blinked in time with her heartbeat, slow, patient, and devastating. Her mind drifted back to the first time she broke down in this meadow. Not the current one, suspended in light and code, but the original version. She'd woken up glitching, terrified, unsure of where the world ended and she began.

Back then, she ran. This time, her feet didn't move.

The prompt waited:

> *Do you wish to finalize the world?*

Reina lowered her gaze to her hands. The same hands that had coded Kaelith's first combat line. The same hands that had dragged assets into a blank scene at three in the morning, whispering, *"Just one more patch. Just make him work."*

She swallowed hard.

Kaelith was still there but barely. He was flickering like he might vanish if she blinked too long. His form jittered at the edges, caught between presence and erasure. The tether between them didn't glow anymore. It simply *existed, faintly*, quiet and expectant like a heartbeat with no guarantee of rhythm.

211

She looked up at the sky that was still white, still soft, and still waiting.

"I don't want clean anymore," she whispered. "I want messy. I want risk. I want something that chooses me back."

And her gaze fell on Kaelith. Even now, on the verge of deletion, he didn't ask her for anything. That was the cost. He wasn't a placeholder. He was a person. But only if she allowed him to become one.

SYRIN's voice returned, gentle but impersonal:

"Root Access may destabilize all tethered entities. You may proceed. Or you may revert."

Reina walked toward the console, her boots echoing with each step like punctuation marks in unfinished code.

She stopped just before the prompt. Her reflection swam in the glass surface. Not the girl who built this world. Not the broken version who ran from it.

But the one who stayed. The one who came back.

"I'm not afraid of losing control anymore," she said softly.

She reached for the console and typed the first two words.

> RUN PROTOCOL:

Reina stared at the blinking cursor, the phrase waiting to be completed. Her fingers hovered over the console. Behind her, Kaelith stood unmoving but still flickering, still fragile, and still entirely present. Not as a prompt. Not as code but as a possibility.

Her heart pounded.

"Do you wish to finalize the world?" the system had asked.

But Reina realized now, this wasn't just about the world. It was about finalizing herself.

Finishing what she began not when she started the game, but when she first asked,

"What if someone didn't leave?"

She thought about *Safe Mode*. About SYRIN's comfort disguised as captivity. About every ghost file that whispered, *"You weren't enough."*

And then, she thought about Kaelith.

About how he stepped forward even when he was breaking. About how he asked to be chosen. Not remembered. Not programmed. But chosen.

Her breath hitched. She looked down.

The prompt waited.

> *RUN* PROTOCOL:

She inhaled.

And typed the final word:

SOULBUILD`

The console didn't flash like the others had.

It glowed. Soft at first, then brighter, as if the command had been waiting all this time. Waiting for her to stop running, to finally believe she didn't need to reset to be worthy of building.

SYRIN's voice spoke one last time, not cold but... reverent.

> *"Protocol   SOULBUILD   acknowledged.*
> *Root   overwrite   initializing.*
> *Emotional   architecture   accepted.*
> *Tether   integrity: preserved.*
> *User choice: complete."*

The world didn't shatter. It exhaled.

Around her, the white light began to shift, threads of color unfurling across the horizon like dawn breaking through rendered fog. The frozen grass warmed. The glitch-clouds began to resolve. From the edges of reality, trees grew, slow and deliberate, as if this world was learning how to live again.

Kaelith's form flickered violently once, then steadied. He looked at her, not with glowing eyes or perfect code, but as someone meeting her halfway. Reina stepped toward him, hands open.

"You're still here," she breathed.

"I always was," he answered softly.

And this time, he reached for her. No prompts. No tether commands. Just touch. Their fingers brushed.

The golden thread returned, glowing brightly, not between them but *around* them. A soft ring of light encircling their joined hands, pulsing like a heartbeat rewritten from scratch.

Behind them, the console blinked for the last time.

[SYSTEM REWRITE: INITIATED]

[REALM: UNSTABLE BUT EVOLVING]

[CORE USER: EMOTIONAL SYNC — TRUE]

Reina exhaled, a smile breaking through tears she hadn't realized were falling.

This wasn't the game she started. It was the one she chose. The one that let her love, glitch and all.

And as the world around them pulsed into its first real breath, Kaelith whispered,

"What happens now?"

Reina looked around—unfinished trees, broken code blooming into flowers, sky rewritten in brushstrokes.

And smiled.

"Now," she said, "we build something worth staying for and hope it stays real."

Chapter 23: If I Wrote You, I'd Still Choose You

"She didn't want control anymore — just connection."

For the first time in a while, the world really breathed.

Reina stood beneath a sky she didn't recognize—half watercolor dawn, half unfinished sketch. The horizon bent in soft angles, like the code wasn't fully rendered but was *learning* from her heartbeat. Trees blossomed mid-motion. Some paused, glitching gently, then decided to bloom anyway. Grass unraveled beneath her boots like ribbon, not from memory files but from her feelings.

Her HUD pulsed softly:

[REALM STATUS: EMOTIONAL ECHO BUILD — LIVE MODE]

[USER CORE ACTIVE | STABILITY: FLUX]

[ALL TETHERED ENTITIES: RECOGNIZED]

She turned, slowly.

Kaelith was behind her, not flickering anymore, not glitching but cautious. His form held steady now, the raw crackle of corruption no longer visible across his joints. But something in his stance gave him away. The way his boots barely pressed into the ground. The way his hands stayed at his sides, like someone waiting for permission to be present.

He wasn't broken. He was afraid of being forgotten.

Reina's chest pulled tight. The world around them shimmered in response, the sky blooming in streaks of gold and blue. Color warped with her breath. Data bent with her ache. This new reality—*Soulbuild*—didn't just respond to logic anymore. It moved with her.

Kaelith's voice came quiet.

"This place… it's made from you."

She nodded, eyes scanning the unfinished forest forming across the hills.

"It's still building. Based on everything I feel."

She walked toward him slowly. Not with urgency, but with intent. His face was still obscured beneath his visor, but his body leaned slightly toward her. Waiting.

"I know what I said at the console," Reina said, her voice barely above a whisper. "But you deserve to hear it again. Not as a system prompt. Not as a goodbye."

Kaelith stayed still, letting the moment stretch.

She inhaled.

"You were meant to be a placeholder, but you changed me. You became more and gave me a reason to become better and let go of the guilt."

The sky pulsed faintly as though listening, a soft ripple of emotion syncing with code.

Kaelith stepped forward, boots pressing into the newly formed ground. The grass accepted him without flicker. He is stable now. Real. At least as real as anything born from love and code could be.

He lifted his head slightly.

Reina's heart pounded. Around them, a stream curved itself from light. The trees swayed in rhythm with her pulse. The entire world waited for her answer.

She stepped closer. Her voice broke.

"Even if this world forgets you," she whispered, "I won't."

The sky opened in that moment, not into void, but into light. And somewhere in the newly forming realm, a path opened.

The path wasn't made of stone or dirt. It formed beneath Reina's steps in real time with soft terrain unfurling like pages from an unwritten book. The trees around them whispered in static sighs, not quite wind, not quite silence. It was as if the entire world was holding its breath, learning how to become the world she wanted as she moved through it.

Kaelith walked beside her now. Still steady. Still quiet. His visor caught the light of the sky, reflecting golds and blues that hadn't existed in the build before. He was no longer just reacting to her; he was matching her pace. Listening and present as always.

But neither of them spoke because there were no words strong enough yet for what this place had become or what it was still trying to be. Not even Reina understood what it was transforming into.

Her HUD shimmered faintly:

[USER EMOTION GRID: ACTIVE — FINAL SYNC LEVEL NEARING]

[RDF CONTAINMENT: FULL — TRANSFER AVAILABLE]

[CORE WORLD STABILITY: 76% AND RISING]

Each line pulsed softly in the corner of her vision, almost like a suggestion. A reminder.

Reina paused on a ridge that overlooked a glimmering canyon of incomplete light. The colors swirled like thoughts she hadn't fully formed. Beneath it, the roots of the new world reached downward, forming bridges between past choices and future possibilities.

Kaelith stopped beside her, still silent.

"You're stable now," she murmured, not looking at him. "But I don't know how long the system will let that last."

He nodded once.

"Stability is not the same as permanence."

She finally turned to him.

"If I could promise you forever, I would."

His voice came quiet.

217

"I don't want forever."

That surprised her. Her brows pulled together slightly.

"You don't?"

He shook his head slowly.

"I want a beginning. *One I get to choose."*

Her breath caught again. Around them, the canyon rippled with soft bursts of golden light. Small arcs of data danced across the sky, like constellations rewriting themselves.

"I collected every RDF in this world," she whispered. "Love, Grief, Defiance, Hope, Regret, Vulnerability…"

Her HUD confirmed it:

[EMOTION GRID COMPLETE — TRANSFER POSSIBLE TO TETHERED ENTITY]

Kaelith turned to her, for the first time not as her protector, not as a function of code, but as someone she'd come to love.

"What will you do with it?" he asked.

She looked at him fully now.

"I want to give it to you."

He blinked in awe.

"That would change everything."

"I know," she said. "But you've changed me. You made me want to stay. To feel. To build something I didn't want to erase, and with you I've learned to be better. It's time you feel too. Time to be your entity and not to exist as code. Time to be able to make your choices."

The world beneath their feet shimmered again. And the golden thread that had returned at the end of the Soulbuild protocol pulsed with radiant intensity.

Reina reached for the console node forming between them, thin strands of code arcing upward from the ground, shaped by her intention. It wasn't a terminal. It wasn't mechanical. It looked like a bloom made of memory. A vessel for trust.

"I want you to feel everything I felt," she said. "Not because I programmed it. But because you earned it."

The world, once coded by isolation, now opened, ready for the next step.

The air shimmered with anticipation.

Above them, clouds began to form and drift, not rendered or looped, but responding to her. To them.

The world wasn't waiting on code anymore. It was waiting on feelings. That was what she made it capable of.

Kaelith stood before her like a question she already knew the answer to, one she had never been brave enough to say aloud.

Reina lifted both hands.

The console-node, hovering between them, pulsed with potential. Gold and silver code strands flowed outward like open circuitry, waiting to be connected. Her HUD pinged softly, once.

[Emotion Grid: Transfer Ready]

[Recipient: Tethered Entity - KAELITH.EXE]

[Warning: Permanent Override – Recipient may evolve beyond original parameters]

Her hands trembled.

This wasn't just a final mechanic. It was a surrender. She was about to give him everything—the love, the pain, the fear, the fight. Every emotion she had unlocked. Every vulnerability she had coded into her journey. Everything to make him more real and human. Not just a code.

Kaelith looked at her, steady.

"You don't have to."

She met his gaze.

"I want to."

He didn't move.

"Then I'll accept. But not because I was made to."

Her eyes burned with emotion.

"I know."

She reached forward. The strands of the Emotion Grid responded immediately. One by one, they flowed into the core that had taken shape within his chestplate, an open aperture of light, like a heart she hadn't written but always hoped he'd grow.

Each emotion entered like a stream:

Hope — the warmth of standing back up after everything tried to break you.

Grief — the weight of memories you can't delete, even when they hurt.

Regret — the hollow that only truths too late can fill.

Defiance — the fire that refused to settle for silence.

Vulnerability — the courage to let someone see you fall apart.

Love — the feeling that made her come back when everything told her to walk away.

As the last thread poured into him, Kaelith's body shuddered with the kind of tremor that felt like awakening. His visor glowed softly, and for the first time since his creation, Reina saw a flicker of emotion behind the mask. Not written or coded but real.

Kaelith blinked slowly, then raised his hand to his chest.

"It's... loud," he said. "Everything you felt. All at once."

"I know," she whispered. "That's what being human feels like."

And at that moment, the tether between them wasn't golden anymore. It became a circle. A loop of light that encased them both, not as creator and creation, but as equals.

Kaelith looked at her, overwhelmed but present.

"If I was made from your pain..." he said slowly, "why does it feel like peace?"

Her breath caught.

"Because I let you become more than what I feared," she said. "You brought peace."

The circle of light around them began to pulse.

Once. Twice. Then it expanded slowly and deliberately, rippling out like an emotional shockwave coded directly from Reina's heart. The world around them responded. Trees flickered, not into default assets, but into new forms—asymmetrical, imperfect, and organic. The sky split into gradients she'd never programmed. Colors she'd never named bled across the clouds.

The world was becoming hers for real.

And Kaelith... was still standing.

His form was no longer flickering. Not fully stable either but gradually evolving. As if her grid wasn't syncing him... it was writing him forward.

"I feel... full," he said, voice low with awe. *"But not overloaded. Just... whole."*

She stepped closer, tears slipping down her cheek.

"Then you're becoming."

He reached for her hand, slowly, reverently. Their fingers laced.

"I don't know what I'll be tomorrow," he said. "I don't even know what I am now. But I know one thing."

Her voice shook. "What?"

Kaelith's gaze, behind the visor, behind the glitches, settled on her.

"If I'm only real because you feel something... then I choose to exist wherever that feeling goes."

Her breath hitched.

"Even if this world forgets me," he continued, "even if I'm overwritten, even if this entire system collapses, I'll know that once, I was chosen."

Reina's heart cracked open.

"You are. You were."

The system around them began to warp again. Not to collapse or reboot. Just… *breathe*. Like the world itself had taken its first inhale after years of waiting.

The HUD blinked:

[CORE   WORLD   STATUS: EVOLVING]
    [COMPANION   FILE: LIVE-EMOTION   THREAD ANCHORED]
        [SOULBUILD   PROTOCOL: ACTIVE]
    [EMOTION GRID TRANSFER: COMPLETE]

Kaelith took one final step forward. No prompts. No commands.

"What happens next?" he asked again. This time, not with doubt but with curiosity.

Reina glanced at the shifting horizon, where the world was writing itself into something new.

And then she looked back at him, her first creation, her most unpredictable glitch, her only choice that had ever felt like love.

She smiled, soft and true.

"Now," she said, "we make a world where no one has to be written to matter."

Above them, the last of the white sky broke open. Not with lightning or code but with light.

And in its center, two figures stood—hand in hand, tetherless, but connected. One who had built the world. One who had rewritten her.

And together, they stepped forward into a new reality—crafted not from safety, not from rules, but from choice.

The last HUD notification blinked across the screen:

[SYSTEM THREAD: EMOTION GRID = HUMANIZED]
[REALM: ALIVE]
[PLAYER PRESENCE: ACCEPTED]
ENDING MODE: USER-DEFINED]

Chapter 24: Realm v2.0 Initialized

"In the end, it wasn't code that trapped her. It was memory."

Reina didn't wake with a start. There was no jolt, no system alert, and no flickering HUD to force her into consciousness.

She simply… breathed.

Warmth met her skin like sunlight through soft gauze. Not the sterile light of rendered skies, but something gentler. She opened her eyes to find a horizon she didn't recognize. Not quite blue, not quite gold, just color suspended in gradients of feeling. The clouds drifted like they had never been coded, just born. Wisps shaped like ideas, like memories trying to become tangible.

She blinked slowly, then sat up. The grass beneath her wasn't perfect. Some blades were too long and others curled at odd angles. But it was soft, warm, and real in a way she'd never programmed. When she pressed her palm to it, there was texture, not the uniform repetition of assets, but the uneven, grounding chaos of life.

No HUD blinked in her vision. No system pinged for attention. No commands, no SYRIN, no tether pulsing in her chest.

Only her. In a realm that didn't ask her to fix anything.

Above her, birds chirped. Not on loop but different songs, with different rhythms. One missed a note. Another stopped mid-call and never finished. It made her laugh. Quietly. Her voice sounded strange in the stillness. Like it didn't have to fight with code to be heard.

She breathed again.

The air smelled faintly of warm earth, the kind that had been touched by rain but not drowned in it. Her body felt whole. Not light like something had been taken away but light like she had finally put something down.

Her fingers brushed the ground again.

No loading texture. No looping animation.

Just... *grass. Real grass.*

Reina stood slowly, knees creaking, and looked around. The meadow was wider than she remembered. Softer, too. The trees nearby didn't grow in straight lines anymore. They twisted as if reaching toward the sound of her breath. Their leaves shimmered in greens that shifted tone every few seconds, not from error, but as if they were unsure what shade matched her mood.

There was no fear here. No urgency. Just curiosity.

She turned slowly in place, taking it all in.

This wasn't a build. It wasn't a patch. It was a beginning.

And she was still here.

Her lips parted, voice low and wonder-struck.

"...Is this what it feels like to belong in one's story?"

A breeze answered, warm and weightless, brushing past her cheek like the world had been listening.

And in that moment, for the first time since the game began, Reina didn't feel like a developer, or a user, or even a survivor.

She just felt human.

Reina stepped forward, unsure if the ground would rise to meet her.

It did. Not with the perfection of code, but the trust of a world learning to walk beside her. The soil was firm beneath her boots but left impressions like it wanted to remember her path.

Around her, the realm continued to unfold not as a map but as a response. Trees grew as she neared them. Wildflowers bloomed in her shadow, uncertain at first, then bold. The sunlight shifted from amber to soft lavender and back again, as if the sky was syncing with the quiet ache in her chest.

This place looked like Evorealm.

But it wasn't.

There were echoes, terrain formations she recognized, cliffs and groves and paths she had rendered in Alpha builds. But they were changed. Slightly tilted. Softer. As though the world had been sketched over by someone who understood her better now than she ever did then.

A shallow stream appeared at the foot of a hill, water trickling over stones that shimmered in too many colors to be natural. They weren't natural. But they were hers. A glitch in the old build would have flagged the variance. Here, the stream sang with it.

Still no HUD. No prompt. No ambient music file on loop. All alone without Kaelith.

Only the heartbeat of a world making itself up as it went.

She ran a hand through her hair and exhaled slowly. Her heart was heavy.

"Kaelith?" Her voice was heavy, yet there was no response. "S-SYRIN?" She called softly, not because she wanted instructions but because she wanted to know if she was alone again.

The breeze paused.

For a moment, nothing happened.

Then, in the space between thought and silence, a voice echoed, not from her mind, not from the world, but from memory, from the very architecture of the realm itself. SYRIN's voice, but gentler than it had ever been. Clear. Not in her ears, but everywhere.

"You finished the story," it said. *"Now live the next one."*

Reina's breath caught.

She didn't respond. Not because she didn't have words, but because none would have done it justice.

This wasn't a command. It wasn't a last directive. It was a farewell.

And it landed like a gift. A blessing from the code that once tried to cage her. Now freed, just as she had freed herself.

She closed her eyes.

"I don't need a system to guide me anymore," she whispered. "I'm ready to feel it all. Even when it hurts."

The realm didn't respond with celebration or confirmation. Instead, it exhaled again.

The light shifted across her skin. The wind danced through her hair. Leaves rustled without loops. For once, this wasn't about saving anything. It was about staying.

Staying to see what came next. She found herself walking.

Not with urgency. There was no threat here, but with memory guiding her feet more than sight. The new world shimmered softly in the corners of her vision, forming landscapes as if answering the silent maps inside her heart. Her steps led her through trees with trunks that shimmered faintly with emotional echoes and past stones carved with glyphs she never wrote but recognized anyway.

Eventually, she came to a clearing.

A meadow, wider than the one before, with hills that sloped gently like the start of a dream. The grass here was wild and real, not simulated. Wind moved it in honest waves. The light kissed the edges of the flowers as they reached toward the sky. It felt... full.

And empty.

There was no one here. Not even a glitch. But her eyes went straight to the center of the clearing. Something small. Something blue. Her chest squeezed.

She stepped closer.

There, in the middle of the softest grass, lay a single object: a ribbon. Blue, frayed at the edges, fluttering gently in the wind like a forgotten bookmark in an unfinished story. It looked like something rendered too carefully to be random. Something chosen.

Her knees gave way before she could stop them. She knelt beside the ribbon and reached for it with trembling hands. The texture was soft. Not coded silk, not placeholder mesh. Just... fabric. Real. Tangible.

Kaelith had held a ribbon like this once, in an old abandoned skin variant she designed years ago and never implemented. He'd only worn it once, in a corrupted dream state during a memory loop when he said, *"If I ever leave, you'll find me by what I choose to leave behind."*

She hadn't remembered that line until now.

Her fingers curled around the ribbon. She didn't sob. She didn't scream. She just... closed her eyes. The wind shifted slightly.

He wasn't here.

No tether. No code thread. No glitched presence behind her.

Just this. His mark. Her hands trembled around the fabric.

"Of course you didn't stay," she whispered. "You were always more idea than instruction."

But the ache that followed didn't hurt like loss. It hurt like love. He hadn't been erased. He had evolved. And whatever this new world was, he had trusted her enough to leave her with the first note in the next story.

The one she'd have to write on her own. She held the ribbon to her heart and let the silence press gently against her skin. He wasn't beside her anymore, but he wasn't gone either. The realm around her shimmered like it was waiting.

Reina stood slowly, the ribbon still cradled in her palm. No prompt appeared. No system chime. No AI voice to guide her next move.

For the first time since this entire journey began, there was no one watching or correcting her choices. No tether guiding her forward. No grid calculating her next emotional beat.

Just a world.

New. Breathing. Unwritten. And hers.

She tucked the ribbon gently into the side of her belt, letting the soft blue fabric rest there, not as a relic, but as a reminder of what she chose. Of who she became. Of who she loved.

The sky above her had settled into a quiet blush with rose gold and lilac layered like the afterglow of something holy. The light no longer shimmered with fragility. It pulsed with invitation.

And somewhere deep in the atmosphere, like a final echo across miles of rebuilt code, SYRIN's voice drifted into her thoughts.

Not commanding or clinical. Just… still.

"You finished the story. Now live the next one."

She smiled, even as tears welled again. This time, not for grief but for fullness.

She had lived inside systems. Built worlds. Lost herself in logic. Let her emotions fracture the foundation of what she thought control was supposed to look like. But she wasn't here to control anymore. She was here to feel.

She turned toward the horizon. The terrain responded by shifting like thought, like emotion, like a realm learning to listen to her heartbeat. The first step forward left no command trail. No error logs. Just footprints in grass made real by belief.

Her HUD didn't return. But she didn't need it now. The code wasn't the interface anymore. She was.

Her hands flexed gently at her sides, and for the first time, she realized they weren't trembling. Not from fear or fatigue. They were just still.

She exhaled. A slow, steady breath. And whispered to herself, to the world, to whoever or whatever might still be listening:

"Let's see what kind of world I can build now."

The light bent ahead of her, forming a gentle path. One not lit by logic trees or story flags but by choice. Honest, human, unfinished choice.

She took one step. Then another.

And the world responded. Behind her, nothing shattered.

Nothing glitched. Only mirrored possibility.

Chapter 25: Welcome, Administrator

"Some worlds are too beautiful to log out of."

Reina stirred slowly, not from disruption, but from stillness so complete it felt sacred. No alert. No tether. No hum of system functions resuming. Just light.

Golden warmth painted the curve of her cheek, soft as breath. It kissed her eyelids before she opened them. For a moment, she didn't move. Just lay there in the hush of morning and let the feeling wrap around her like waking up inside someone's dream, where nothing had to be perfect to be beautiful.

When she did rise, it was gentle. Her fingers curled into the grass beneath her. They were cool, damp with dew, and delightfully imperfect. One blade curled into a loop. Another bent under its own weight. No asset symmetry. No repeating texture grid. Just grass.

She sat up fully, eyes scanning the world that had formed around her.

Mist clung low to the valley ahead, parting like a curtain drawn by intention rather than breeze. In the distance, where soft hills met a new horizon, she saw it—a town. One she didn't recognize. Compact rooftops. Arched windows. Warm stone with smoke rising from tiny chimneys that puffed without code repetition.

Her breath caught in her chest, but not out of fear.

The world hadn't reset. It hadn't collapsed. It had... changed. Not into something better. Not into something clean but into something new.

Her hands moved instinctively toward her vision, expecting the HUD to blink awake, expecting system overlays or notifications. But nothing came. No emotional syncs. No tether alerts. Just her hands. Human and solid.

And for the first time, she didn't panic at the silence. Instead, she breathed.

The air smelled of ashwood and distant river water. A bird sang nearby—off-key, cheerful, and unlooped. The sky above her pulsed with morning colors that felt like possibility. She turned her head slowly, soaking in every detail.

There were no landmarks she'd designed. No flagged spawn zones. No residual glitches. Just terrain that unfolded like a story written by emotion rather than command.

She stood.

Her boots left indentations in the dirt, shallow and soft. The earth wasn't calculating her coordinates anymore. It was feeling her presence.

As she took a step forward, she felt it again. The memory. Not just of what she'd lost but what she'd learned. Her burnout. Her breakdown. Her fear of being the one who always had to fix everything. And yet... here she was. Whole. Rooted. Not in control, but finally, undeniably *in tune*.

She didn't need a console. She didn't need to look back.

The town ahead shimmered in the distance, waking slowly like her. It waited, not like a quest hub, but like a welcome. And beneath her ribs, where the tether once glowed, something new stirred.

Not a connection. The feeling of a new beginning.

Reina began walking.

Not with urgency, not like someone chasing closure, but like someone learning how to exist again. Her footsteps were light, but every press of her boots into the soil felt intentional, like the world registered each movement as a new declaration:

I'm still here. I'm choosing to stay.

The path didn't appear beneath her like old navigation triggers. It was already there, worn faintly, dusted with petals from a nearby bloom tree. The flowers were soft pink and pale coral, their scent drifting lazily in the air. She reached out and brushed one as she passed. The petal responded by curling slightly, a detail too subtle to have been programmed.

It was responding to her.

The sky had shifted from gold to warm rose. Sunlight filtered through clouds with no repetition. They drifted as if thinking, reshaping with feeling rather than function. The wind came next, a soft gust that tangled in her hair, not to move her but to remind her that the world breathed now. Just like she did.

And Reina... didn't feel alone.

She was alone, physically. Kaelith wasn't by her side. There was no tether brushing her chest, no gentle static that signaled his proximity. But the ache didn't hollow her like it once would have. Instead, it filled her gently, like a memory made of light.

The ribbon he left was still tied at her hip, fluttering with every step. She didn't know if she'd ever see him again. But that was the difference now. She could keep going without breaking.

Each footstep brought her closer to the town on the horizon. As she drew near, she noticed details: a windmill on the ridge, spinning slowly and unevenly. Lanterns that swung gently even though no breeze touched them. A wooden bridge crossing a narrow brook, where fish swam in awkward loops, not coded to impress, just... *alive.*

A group of villagers were just beginning to stir. NPCs? Maybe. But not like before.

These ones weren't looping idle animations. They laughed. Whispered. One knelt to tie her sandal. Another bent over to sweep the front of a shop that had no name yet. It wasn't their dialogue that made Reina stop. It was their *presence*. They moved like people. They looked like people.

And none of them looked like something she'd made. Which meant something new had begun to create alongside her.

A small boy ran past her, holding a bundle of cloth shaped like a fox. He paused for a heartbeat, looked up at her with wide eyes, then smiled before darting off again. The ribbon at her hip caught his gaze briefly, but he said nothing. Didn't question her.

She wasn't a dev here. She was just... someone. Reina took a slow breath and kept walking. The town wasn't waiting to be built. It had already begun.

As Reina stepped deeper into the town, a soft hum rose from somewhere within her, like old memories stirring in the marrow of her bones.

The village was alive, not in the sense of activity but awareness. Each corner she turned felt like it had been waiting for her. Not to test her or to trap her but to witness her presence. Cobblestone paths stretched out with uneven patterns. Some stones glowed faintly under her steps, as if marked by distant echoes of places she'd once imagined but never fully built.

A bakery stood at the town's edge, and the scent of something sweet, berries, maybe cinnamon, drifted into the air. A windchime above the door played a melody she didn't recognize, but it felt familiar, like something she might've composed late at night and deleted before sunrise. A girl stood at the window, sketching with chalk on the pane. She glanced up and nodded at Reina, not with scripted politeness but with silent acknowledgment.

Reina nodded back.

Each interaction felt like a new patch of soul meeting old code. Her chest ached tenderly. Her emotions were no longer raw or wild. They were settling, like dust after a long collapse.

And beneath it all, the memories resurfaced. They weren't sharp or invasive this time. They came gently.

She remembered coding for seventeen hours straight on a project she didn't believe in. Remembered eating dinner at her keyboard. Falling asleep to glowing error messages. Crying quietly when another update broke her build.

She remembered SYRIN's earliest voice. Lines meant to be reassuring, clean, and robotic perfection. She remembered deleting her first companion build because it wasn't "compelling" enough. How she second-guessed every design. Every choice.

She remembered Kaelith's early sketches. How she once called him "a beautiful waste of time." And how, somewhere in the quiet moments she didn't notice, he became the reason she stayed.

She paused outside a glass shop with warped panes and crooked walls. It shimmered under the morning light, and she caught her reflection in the window.

For the first time… she saw all of herself. Not just the developer or the burnout. Not just the girl who wanted to make something beautiful. But the woman who had.

And then… she heard it.

A voice.

Faint. Passing.

"Hello, Traveler."

She turned sharply. Her heart clenched.

The man who spoke was already walking away, his back turned. He wore a simple coat. Brown boots. His gait was steady, unremarkable.

But the tone. The voice. It scratched at her ribs. Not in fear. In recognition.

"Wait—" she called, voice cracking. She stepped forward.

But he didn't stop. Didn't run either. He kept walking. The ribbon at her side caught the wind and fluttered toward him.

He didn't turn back. But her heart did.

Reina stood frozen for a heartbeat longer than she meant to. The sound of the voice still echoed through her chest like a bell struck at her center. Something in it had wrapped around her ribs. Like possibility. She glanced down at the ribbon tied to her belt. It had stilled, as if listening too.

She didn't chase him. Didn't call out again.

Somehow, she knew if it was him, really him, then he didn't need to be followed. He had walked away not to disappear… but to let her stay.

The wind brushed past her, and in it came the faintest trace of warmth.

Presence. The kind that leaves you a little changed, even when nothing around you looks different. She turned back toward the town. It was beginning to bustle now. NPCs—if they could still be called that, moved with intention and grace. A child laughed as he spilled a bag of floating fruit. A merchant repaired a sign with glowing nails. A woman hummed a tune with no loop, as though improvising existence itself.

None of it felt like a script. None of it felt like something she'd written. And maybe that's what made it so real.

For the first time, the world was alive, not just reacting to her emotions but building alongside them. Not from perfection or the need to control but from trust.

She walked on, quietly.

Her boots made soft thuds against the earth, and every step left a mark the world chose to keep.

The town unfolded without fanfare, buildings of odd symmetry, and bridges that curved not for efficiency but for beauty. Glitches didn't vanish here; they adapted. Colors shifted based on proximity to people's laughter. Doors didn't lead to the same place twice.

And yet, there was peace.

She paused at a fountain in the square.

The water didn't loop. It danced. And her reflection in it smiled back, not with triumph, not with perfection, but with presence. She was here. Fully.

And then it came. Not through her HUD but somewhere deeper, where narrative used to live and where choice had now taken root.

A final system line, whispered like a closing stanza of a long-forgotten poem:

[System status: Memory Code restored.]

[Administrator synced.]

[Reboot complete.]

The words weren't commands. They weren't limitations. They were a welcome.

A single, silent confirmation that everything—the glitches, the grief, the tethered love, the breaking, and staying—had led her here. Not to an ending but to her beginning.

She stepped back from the fountain and looked toward the horizon again, now tinged with the first brush of amber morning.

And for once, the world didn't ask her to run.

It invited her to walk.

To build. To belong. To live.

The light curved forward like the start of a sentence never written before, and Reina smiled.

As the screen faded softly to black.

www.ingramcontent.com/pod-product-compliance
Lightning Source LLC
Chambersburg PA
CBHW022136240626
47153CB00007B/2384